"They haven't got one clue about where we are, not one. We could be in South America for all anybody knows."

"Let em suffer," Curtis said.

That's what we was doing all right, letting them suffer. Especially Curtis' old man. Good enough for him. He deserved to suffer for a change. Find out what it's like to be getting the dirty end of the stick. Having to take it now instead of dishing it out. That'll make the old man think twice. Make him learn the hard way that this stupid yelling and roughing up don't work all the time.

And then I started thinking—who was I to be talking?

KEVIN MAJOR, a native of Newfoundland, is the editor of *Doryloads,* an anthology of local folk literature. *Hold Fast* is his first novel.

HOLD FAST

KEVIN MAJOR

LAUREL-LEAF BOOKS bring together under a single imprint outstanding works of fiction and nonfiction particularly suitable for young adult readers, both in and out of the classroom. Charles F. Reasoner, Professor Emeritus of Children's Literature and Reading, New York University, is consultant to this series.

Published by
Dell Publishing
a division of
Bantam Doubleday Dell Publishing Group, Inc.
666 Fifth Avenue
New York, New York 10103

This work was first published in Canada by
Clarke, Irwin & Company Limited.

ISBN: 0-440-93756-6

RL: 4.3
Reprinted by arrangement with Delacorte Press
Printed in the United States of America
September 1981

10   9   8

KRI

PART
ONE

1

I'm going to start off this way so I can get the hardest part over with first. Then I won't have to be thinking about it so much later on. I can maybe tell it better that way.

The worst of it all was in the graveyard. The church part was hard enough, but the graveyard. . . . I don't think I'll ever have to face on anything that bad again.

I said afterwards that if the minister'd never been so long getting ready and getting the words out then maybe I wouldn't a bawled. But I knows that's not really the truth. I just couldn't keep from doing it. Just no way in the world could I keep it in. Not with them going down into the gravel like that. Slow as anything. Like the coffins would never make it down to the bottom.

I must a shook my head a dozen times to drive the damn stuff away. And I stood there then, soft as mud, bawling my eyes out. Water pouring out like nobody'd ever died before. The others just stood around like a bunch of dummies. Thinking,

I knew, that me crying was all a part of it. A son is expected to bawl his head off when his parents die. No matter how old he is.

And then part way through, it got so bad that I just couldn't stick it anymore. I had to tear outa there. And just as fast as I could, I took off in front of all the people, every one of them turning to me with stupid-looking pity in their eyes. Past all the headstones, down in through the woods. As far as I could get outa their sight. Across the paths where the skidoos use to go. I ran like hell's flames. Getting away from it. Ran till I was that far away it was like none of them would ever get the chance to see me again.

Run, I thought to myself, don't stop. Stop and it'll ram right into your mind and never get out again.

That looks like a good rabbit's path, so tail a slip there, he'd a said. Said.

Run. Run, you crazy fool of a son. Run through the paths. Jump outa the way or them thoughts'll grab ya! Bring ya up all-standin. Choke ya. Take away your last livin breath, clean and holy.

It's no good. Holy God, I thought, it's no good! They're dead. The two of them are gone. Gone and dead and buried.

When it got dark I ended up at the beach on Mercer's Point. For no sensible reason I was on the beach, shivering. Being there after dark wasn't like me. Except maybe if it was the middle of the summer or something, at a party. But none of that mattered anymore. It wasn't worth a lousy thing.

I closed my eyes and it was all still banging into my brain. I opened them and looked out on the salt water. That was the only thing that made any sense. For sure that was always going to come back in. All the time slapping up on the sand and the rocks.

I tried to think of something else. Other things, like salmon fishing, the holidays and the swimming, the caplin when they rolled right up on that same beach a week before. Thousands of fish piling over each other, flicking like mad on the sand when the water went out, flicking to get washed back out with the next wave. Scravelling to stay alive.

But it didn't work this time. Made it worse. The banging didn't stop. Wouldn't either, till I cut out trying to fool myself and looked at it straight.

It came to me about the time he sliced open his arm with the chain saw. I bawled then too. "Shut up your damn foolishness," he yelled, "and help me!" I threw down the axe and done what he said—hauled off his coat and sweater and shirt, down to where the saw had ripped into his arm. The muscle was all open in the freezing cold, blood streaming out until I had the other shirt sleeve tied and twisted around his arm, like he told me to do. "Now get the skidoo started and let's get home outa this." It was the fastest I ever drove the skidoo. I had her right tight to the handle bars almost the whole way out. "Give it to er, give it to er!" he yelled. Him on behind with one arm wrapped around my waist and one sleeve of the coat flapping in the wind. I got us home in the garden safe. A trail of blood for maybe two miles back up in the woods.

A gull flew over the salt water in front of me screeching his bloody lungs out. Just as I had it outa my mind. If I'd a had my .22 I'd a flattened him on right there.

No mercy for those ones.

No mercy for the drunks who drives cars and kills people. Parents of people.

No mercy for the drunken blood-of-a-bitch who drove headlong into their car and got them killed.

I tore out and made for the sand bank. Climbing up it, every time sinking back some, pawing the sand till I reached the grass ground on the top. To where I could still see the salt water slapping up on the landwash.

I backed up from the edge of the bank. I ran and jumped whatever I could go, down the sand bank again. And jumped and jumped. Down the sand, running like a madman, stumbling back to the water.

I came to a stop. I stood up to my ankles in the running water. It plowed in over my shoes full of sand. Then, after a long while, I went back ashore and emptied them. Put my feet back into wet and gritty old shoes.

There was no place to go then. No place atall.

No place left except back to where I was expected to be.

2

By the time I got back near to the house from the beach that night in June, I was pretty well ready to face up to Aunt Flo and anything she might say to me. But then I seen that it wasn't just Aunt Flo I'd have to face, but a whole crowd of others, all ganged up there, just waiting for me to get back. I was in no mood for that. After the funeral and everything, and then to have to come back into my own house and run headlong into all them glaring eyes. I knew a good lot of what was inside had no business there in the first place. Some of them hardly ever set foot in the house before, except when they wanted to borrow something. I had a good mind to tell them to get lost. I didn't want any of their stupid pity.

I came in and took off my shoes in the porch. My socks too, because I didn't want to be trailing water all over the place. The ones inside heard me.

I knew what I was going to have to listen to, as soon as I went through the porch door. Where was you? And all that. And I knew too that give them either bit of a chance atall and they'd be blaring out their sympathy. "That's all right, my boy," and, "It must be hard on a boy that age." I could just see it. Every one of them wanting to get in their two cents worth. Trying to make out like they was going to be some help. Well, I didn't need them. I got along good enough before without their help. I could darn well do the same now.

"Don't say anything. Just leave me alone." And I took off up the stairs to my room.

I took a look at some of them when I went by. For sure that Rita Tucker had to be there. Her and her big mouth. For sure she had to be there if there was anything going on that she could talk about afterwards. She had to be in the centre of it. I should a give her a good piece of my mind. Go home. Go on home and look after your own self. You wasn't so flick to say anything good about me last winter when I went across your stupid land on skidoo. You was quick enough to bawl at me then. Jake Matthews, you too. You can go take your lousy apple trees and burn them for all I cares. We was only having a bit of fun. Batter on home the works of you. Go down to the club and play darts or something. Who needs you?

All right, all right. So they're not all as bad as that. But so what if it's only me and Brent now? So what if I am only fourteen? We don't need anybody.

The only place that I really could go to that

was all mine was my bedroom. But even that place I was fed up with. As soon as I went through the door I wanted to rip down all the junk off the walls, tear down the stupid posters and heave it all away. I took the record player off the desk and shuffed that in the closet and fired the whole darn lot of records in on top of it. And then all the junk on the bureau. I rammed what I could get of it into the drawers. That was the right thing to do— get it outa my sight. It was only foolishness anyway, half of it. I should a dumped the whole bloody lot into the garbage can.

After ten minutes I stretched out across the bed and took a hard look around. On the wall was left a frame full of old Newfoundland coins Grandfather gave me one time. And the gun rack me and Dad done up last year. Every other bloody thing was made away with.

I stayed stretched across the bed like that for a long time. I tried to make myself believe that it was going to be a new start. But not one thing I'd done made me feel any better. It was just as well if I'd come in and jumped on the bed in the first place. And stuck my head in the pillow and not budged an inch. I would a been just as well off.

I could hear the noise of them all downstairs talking. For sure it was about me. It was a strange thing one of them hadn't been up over the stairs before that to see what all the racket was about.

They had to be talking about what was going to happen to me and Brent. If they didn't already have it all figured out, case closed, and all ready to dish out to us. But they might just have to put their thinking caps on again, because this was one fellow who wasn't about to be sent off to somewhere he didn't want to go. They could mark that down. And if there was no one for me to live with, then shag them, I'd live by myself. Or just the two of us together for that matter. I'd soon fix that.

If there was any reason why I couldn't stay in Marten and live with my relatives like I had in my mind to do, then it was because both of them, Grandfather and Aunt Flo, was too old. Grandfather was in his seventies and they lived together, him and Aunt Flo, Dad's sister. Her husband was dead. And she already had one family reared up and gone.

Then there was Mom's sister, Aunt Ellen, who lived in St. Albert. Her and her husband was to the funeral. They didn't live that far away, a few hundred miles, but still I didn't know that much about them. They might a been at our place twice or maybe three times. Uncle Ted and Dad never did get along. They had two children, I knew that much. One fellow about my age.

I thought that if things worked out right then just maybe we'd end up with Aunt Flo. She was a bit of a mother hen, but I could easy enough put up with that if I set my mind to it.

It was Aunt Flo who finally trotted up over the stairs. I knew there had to be someone come up after a while. She came right by the door, but she didn't try to open it.

"Michael, can I come in?"

"No!" I told her. I wasn't ready for that yet.

"I wants to see you."

"What for?"

"Open the door. I wants to see how you are."

"No," I snapped again.

"You must be hungry."

"No, I'm not."

"I bet you are. I'll go get you something to eat." And before I knew it she was gone back down over the stairs. Food—that was always her way of getting to people. Well, she'd need more than food to get me to talk. Even though I never had a bite to eat since that morning.

I was dead set against opening that door, dead set against it. But when she came back up over the stairs and I knew she was waiting outside to be let in, I just didn't have enough rottenness in me to keep her out. I turned the knob. She had a tray in her hands with a sandwich on it and a glass of milk and some buns. I was glad that it was that way—her hands full. I didn't want no scene where she could wrap her arms around me and have me cry.

"Are you feeling all right, Michael?"

"Why shouldn't I be?"

"Michael . . ." She put the tray down on the desk. She looked hard at me, and then I had to look back at her. I could a kicked myself for

opening the door. It all started to come out. About
how she knew it was hard. How she knew it was
very tough on me. She used those words because
she figured it was something I'd use. I couldn't get
mad at her for that. And she did lose a brother.

She said losing a mother and father is worse.
Shit, she didn't have to tell me that. I knew that.
And the lousy way I felt, I knew that too. I knew
that better than she did.

All right. So I bawled again. But I didn't bawl
on her shoulder. And she didn't say anything,
which was all right too. I bawled and shook and
covered my head, the whole stupid show. And I
wasn't ashamed of it. I was not. Not one bit.

After a while, when she went away and left me
alone, I managed to cut it out again. But hungry
as I was and even with the food all there in front
of me, I still couldn't put much of it in my gut. I
just couldn't get it down into me.

There was something else too. If Brent was in
his room, then I knew he must a heard what went
on. His room was just down the hall. He's only
seven, so for a while I figured that maybe he'd
been taken somewhere else to sleep. I opened my
door and walked down towards his. The light
from the hall shone in on his bed. He was there.

I stood up in the doorway and pushed the door
open further. He wasn't asleep. He was lying there
on his back, rolling an empty glass over and over
on his stomach. He looked over towards the light.

I went in and took a chair from the corner of the room and put it by the bed. Backwards, so's I had somewhere for my arms. I put my chin down on my arms and looked at him. For a long time, neither of us spoke to each other.

"I got some plans for tomorrow," I said suddenly. I tried to make it sound like I was excited.

"Why don't we go to sleep?" he said, very quiet.

"Listen. How about we go up in the woods early in the mornin? Just the two of us."

He was looking at me, but he didn't say anything.

"You're always after me to take you in the woods. We'll build a camp." I waited for him to answer.

Then he said, "I don't want one anymore."

"Yes, you do," I told him. "I knows a real good place. No one ever built one there before. Come up and we'll see what you thinks of it."

"I don't want a camp."

"It'll just be the two of us. We'll build it between us and we won't tell anybody a thing about it. Okay?"

"You said before you wouldn't do it."

"That was different. I changed my mind. I wants to now."

"Why?"

"It'll be somethin for us to do—build a camp like you've been asking for all along. We'll make it better than ar other one around. Better than the one Joe Norman and them got build, way better than that. You wouldn't be afraid to sleep in it, would you, Brent?"

"No, I wouldn't be afraid. I'm not afraid of bears."

"Moose?"

"No. Moose wouldn't touch you inside a camp."

"Rats."

"Rats?"

"I was just kiddin. There wouldn't be no rats."

"Wouldn't you be afraid, Mike?"

"Me? Frig no."

"There'd be the two of us, right?"

"Right."

"Could we set out rabbit slips then, in the fall?"

"Yeah, we'll do that."

When I said about the rabbits, it stopped everything. Like it was a sign that something was really screwed up. I spose it came to him right away that I never said yes that easy before, about him and me going after rabbits.

He stopped looking at me. His face got even more serious than it was first when I came in through the door. His lips went together tight.

"Mike."

"Yeah."

"Is you afraid?"

I knew it was that. "A bit afraid," I said.

"A lot?"

"Yeah . . . when I thinks about it."

I could see his eyes starting to fill up.

"I mean, they won't send us away, will they? Like to an orphanage?"

"No, they wouldn't do that."

"Cause if they do, I won't go. Aunt Flo won't send us where we don't want to go, will she?"

"You knows Aunt Flo wouldn't do that."

"She might. She might. Nobody wants us. We got no mudder or no fa . . ."

"Shut up!"

Then the water really started to come.

"I'm sorry. Stop it now. Com'on, stop it. Nobody is goin to take you anywhere."

"You don't know."

"Yes, I do."

"No, you don't."

"Stop your cryin. You're not that big of a baby anymore. Look at ya. Like some two-year-old."

"You're someone to talk. You was bawlin too. I heard ya."

"Shut up. Everybody'll be upstairs if you keeps that up."

"I don't care."

"Shut up!"

He wouldn't stop.

"Cry baby. Cry baby. You big sook!"

"Shut up," he said.

"Cry baby! Sook!"

"Shut up."

"Make me."

"I'll hit ya."

"You might try, sook."

"I said shut up or I'll hit ya good and hard."

"Hit me. Com'on and hit me."

"I really will. Hard."

"Cry baby!"

"Shut up!"

He wrung up his fist.

"Sook!"

And I let him hit me really hard. As hard as he darn well liked.

The next morning the sunlight came pouring in through the bedroom window. The heat spread all over us across the bed. I was already hot and sticky with sweat, stuck and twisted in my clothes. Not so much as a draft all during the night because I never had the mind to get up and open a window. Brent was next to me, sweaty the same way. The poor kid. He cried till I gave up trying to make him stop.

All that night I had tried like crazy to sleep. I had turned in the bed a thousand times. It came back to me, back and back and back to me all night. I got stomach sick. But if I had throwed up my guts it wouldn't a made me any better.

I looked at Brent. "You think it's going to be easy," I said, waking him up. "The hell with you buddy, it's not. Get outa bed. Go get some clean clothes on. Go on."

When Aunt Flo came and looked in the doorway to see if we was awake, she got an awful surprise. I never gave her so much as a chance to say anything. I just told her we'd soon be down to breakfast. Then I hauled on a clean pair of jeans and a red and white T-shirt. One with leaves on it. It was the best one I had. And I made sure that Brent had himself washed good and dressed like I told him to.

See, I'm pig-headed. Dad always said I was pig-headed. No more than he was. Well, I was trying to take all that had happened square in the face. I was trying. They both would a told me to do it that way. They would a said see what you can make of yourself.

It wasn't going to be that easy. Downstairs, me and Brent walked in on a kitchenful of miserable silence. Aunt Flo, Uncle Ted and Aunt Ellen, even Grandfather, neither one of them was saying a word.

"Whas we havin' for breakfast?" I said right away. Loud, like a dish smashing across the middle of the floor.

They sat there dumb. Probably they expected me to bawl for them.

"Any eggs fried?" Loud again.

"Michael, I didn't think you'd want eggs this morning," Aunt Flo said, almost stuttering it out. "I made you some pancakes, just like you likes them. But you wait a minute. If you wants eggs, I'll fry you some. You'll have some too, won't you, Brent?"

"Sure he will," I told her, and looked at Brent

as much as to say that he better not say no, if he
knew what was good for him.

Aunt Ellen and Uncle Ted on the daybed—they
both started to come alive as if I had yanked on
their strings. Like me talking was signal for them
to have something to say.

All kinds of brilliant stuff. "It's a great day on
the water, Michael. I daresay there's a few fish on
the go this morning."

"That's what we should have for dinner, boys—
a good meal of fish." Right full of being normal.

"No odds to us what we haves," I said. "What
we wants to know is if we gotta get outa this
house and where you got in mind for us to go if
we do."

That loused up their fish talk pretty quick. I
could a struck the kitchen with a bulldozer and
they wouldn't a got any more of a shock. I wasn't
about to try to be extra nice about it. No sense
himmin and awin all morning when we all knew
it had to come down to that sometime.

You could just about see their nerves twitching.
Aunt Flo almost dropped the frying pan. The two
on the daybed could barely keep hold of the ciga-
rettes they had nipped between their fingers.
Ashes flying all over the place. It even got Grandfather upset. The rocking chair he was in went off
stride.

"We'll talk about that after breakfast, Michael,"
Aunt Flo said, trying to smooth it all over.

"No sir. We wants to know right now." As

simple as that. I wasn't being brazen about it if that's the way it looked. I just wanted to get it straight right then and there.

"It's better you boys had your breakfast first." That was Uncle Ted. Coming on strong like he was the voice of experience or some big deal.

"What, is it so bad that you can't tell us?"

"Michael," Aunt Flo said, "it's only been one day."

"You mean you haven't talked about it yet?"

"No, I didn't say that."

"Then tell us. I was awake all last night thinkin about it. Brent too."

Then Brent, who hadn't opened his mouth the whole time, said to Aunt Flo, "Is we goin to an orphanage?"

When she heard that she just about broke down crying right there. She came over to the table, stood up by him and squeezed him into her dress. She could hardly keep it in.

"Brentie my love, you knows better than that." Then, in a few seconds, after she got a hold on herself, she said, "Brentie, how would you like to come and live with me and your Grandfather?" She looked at him and pushed his hair back from his forehead.

"Okay," he said right away. A big relief.

And what about me? The other one. The one who is not going to ask. Where does he fit into all this? I was waiting. Feeling stupid, because I didn't want it to look like I was waiting.

"Mike too?" Brent said then.

Nobody answered. Until Aunt Ellen spoke up, all full of life, but not laying her eyes on me atall. "Michael is going to come to live with us in St. Albert."

So that was it. That was what they had in their minds. St. Albert. The least she could a done was look at me when she said it.

"You're going to like it in St. Albert, Michael," Uncle Ted said. Again like he was positive that what he said had to be right.

"Maybe I will."

"I know you will."

"I said maybe I will."

And then a long silence, everybody waiting. Until I said, "I'll give it a try." I said it like I meant it.

3

I had a whole two months before I would be packing up and getting myself shipped off to St. Albert to start school there. Aunt Flo said I could stay with her until then. Maybe she thought that by the end of August I'd have no problem to face on a move.

But I was definitely going. That was understood and there wasn't much more said about it. I knew both of us, me and Brent, living with her was a lot to expect from Aunt Flo. And she had Grandfather, too, to take care of. It would be hard enough on her to cook and wash and spend money on them, let alone me too. So I wasn't about to ask her to change her mind.

It was just that Marten was the best darn place I knew to live. God, what was I talking about, it was the only place I ever did live. Of course, you can almost count the number of people on one hand. Not really, but going by some places in Newfoundland, Marten is pretty small. Probably no more than seven hundred people all together.

But that didn't matter. In fact, I liked it that way cause it gave us all kinds of room to be roaming around. I could put on the boots and leave the back of the house and in no more than two minutes I'd be up in the country, out of sight of any house in the place. Go on all day then, if I wanted, and not see a single soul.

You might think a person would get bored silly with nothing to do in a place that small, but no sir, not me. I can hardly think of a morning when I woke up and there wouldn't be something on my mind that I'd have to look forward to. If it wasn't going in the woods to check my snares after school, it might be riding around on skidoo. Or setting lobster traps. There was times when I bloody near went nuts trying to get some sleep, I'd be planning that much for the next day.

And now my whole life was going to be changed. I just kept thinking to myself that St. Albert better not be as bad as the picture of it I had in my mind.

I got carried away a lot that summer, all the time thinking about things that was gone past and what I would be leaving behind. I should a been planning ahead for when I got to St. Albert instead of moping around in a daydream half the time. I did spend some time out and around with the fellows. Not very much though. Nothing like other summers. In fact, except for some of the times me and Brent spent together, it was the rottenest summer I ever had. Even all the extra baking and stuff Aunt Flo did for us didn't seem to make it any better.

Over the years Aunt Flo and me always got along fairly good, I spose, all things considered. Although for as long as I could remember, she was always the kind of person who fussed over you too much. For one thing, any time I ever went over there, say after school to see Grandfather and maybe have something to eat, she always had to see that I was stuffed right to the gills. No such a thing as one piece of cake. It had to be two or three or she'd figure you didn't like it. And I wouldn't get outside the door but I had my pockets stogged full with oranges or bananas or something.

And sometimes the questions she'd put me through would get right clean on my nerves. I spose it only showed she was worrying about me. I spose that was it. Like if it was either bit cold atall, the first question she'd be sure to put to me was did I have on long underwear. Now, is that any kind of question to get asked you by your aunt? I always said yes, whether I did or not. Lots of times I'd have plenty of things on the tip of my tongue to say to her to cure her of that little habit. But if I ever did and what I said got back to Mom, then I'd a been hung.

After, though, when I moved over and started to live in her house, all that stuff about her I didn't notice so much. She was different. She left me alone a lot. And when I got it in my mind to, I done my part to help her out around the house.

For the two months before I left, I spent most of the time to myself or with Brent. For me, getting along with Brent as good as I done was even stranger than Aunt Flo and me finally seeing eye to eye. Before that the two of us could hardly look at each other sideways but a fight started. It mightn't a been as bad as that, but we sure got into some vicious arguments. Like a lot of younger brothers, he could be a real pain in the neck when he wanted to be. What use to bug me more than anything was when he'd come home to Mom with these stun stories about me. Wherever he got them I don't know. He'd try to make her believe that he seen me smoking or he'd say he heard me curse so bad he couldn't repeat it. Or if he seen me with some girl. That was another thing. Cripes, I warned him about that so many times my tongue had blisters. What he needed most was a good smack on the arse. He came darn close to getting it too, a good many times. He'd only say that stuff about me if we was all around the dinner table or something and he knew I couldn't belt him one.

But that came around to being changed too. It's odd when I thinks about it. How us two could a changed into being pretty good buddies. I spose it all started when I began to feel that I should be looking out to him more. When I knew that something just had to be done about the way he was acting.

I seen that it was even worse for him than it was for me. Being only seven he took it awful hard. Some people got the idea that a kid his age could get over something like what happened in no time. They don't know much if that's what they thinks. I couldn't let him stay like that, so dopey and not interested in doing a thing. Crying every hour almost. I wasn't any rock myself, I'll admit to that. But I was nothing like what Brent was. I was afraid he was going to stay like that all his life.

So I got him talking to me as much as I could. About everything I could think of that I knew he had either bit of interest in. Sometimes it was hard to drag so much as a word outa him. He would just sit there like a dummy and listen to me. Then gradually he started to come around.

"Take that horse Jack Coles got there. He's some animal," I'd say to him. "You like to have a horse like that?"

"Yeah," he might say.

"Now what would you do with en if you had en?"

He'd have to come up with more than just a word or two.

It worked too, enough that I could see a big difference in him. I done all I could to get Brent back to the way he should a been. I'd rather a seen him yelling and screaming at me than for him to be the way he was first.

* * *

By the end of a few weeks he looked and acted a whole lot better. Some nights we'd have a real cuffer. If Mom and Dad could a seen it they probably would a had to laugh to theirselves. There we was, carrying on what you could call a sensible conversation. Neither one of us stretching our lungs the least bit.

What we was talking about this one night was squids. It wasn't quite the right time of the year for them then, but we was on to talking about them anyway. A good evening of squid jigging in September or October is one of the best bits of fun you can have out on the salt water. I've been at it a good many times and I knows a fair bit about it. But Brent, he only ever been out once. Lucky for him though they was jigging good that evening and he had the real time of it.

Most everybody knows I guess what a squid looks like. It's like a pouch with suckers on their arms coming out at one end. Arms like an octopus, only smaller. If anything grabs hold of them, they shoots out this black inky stuff—squid shit.

Now all the fun is in being out jigging them. Around dark in the evening or early in the morning is the best time. A small red squid jigger with a bit of line is all you needs. You don't have to go out very far, only just off the cove. All the boats generally anchors around about in the same spot.

Talk about your fun, old man, when the jiggin's good. We've been out, me and Dad and Grandfather, some evenings when we could a filled the boat. Squid shit going everywhere then, cause as soon as they comes up outa the water, they lets fly. That's half the fun of it—getting squirt, or better still seeing someone else getting their face full.

That's what we was talking about mostly—squids. When Grandfather came in on the two of us cuffering away there in the bedroom, it must a been ten o'clock or later. All the time I was sorta half expecting to see him. It seemed Grandfather was the right one to be in with us all along.

It might seem odd about me and Grandfather, the way we always got along so good. I guess he was a lot of the reason that it would a been at Aunt Flo's that I'd a been staying for good, if I had my own way.

Some fellows I knows haven't got no time for their grandparents. Like they figures it's not very smart to be saying much that's good about them. Or about any old people, for that matter. Like what they thinks or says is too old-fashioned for them. Or maybe it's because the grandparents they got are too contrary. I don't know. But me and Grandfather wasn't one bit like that. We got along great, better than I done with some my own age.

The trouble with a good many old people is that they thinks they was never young. But Grandfather was not that way. He had stories, my son, that'd put some of what you reads in magazines and books to shame. And I knows for a fact they're true. Now and then he might tell one to pull someone's leg, just for fun, but if you had all what happened to him put together, you'd have enough to fill ten books. No joke about it. Sure he went fishing in a sailing schooner on the Labrador every summer for twenty-two years from the time he was thirteen years old. And that was no easy job, that's for darn sure.

You had to know how to go about speaking to Grandfather, too. It was no use to say something to him and be looking out the window or fiddling with whatever was on the table or have your mind half on something else. You had to look right straight at him and talk loud. If you learned that you wouldn't have to go repeating what you was saying to him more than once.

Grandfather's hair's been white ever since I can remember. He use to keep it cut right tight to his head, but late years he took to letting it grow out, that and his sideburns. I told him once he should buy an electric guitar and practise up a bit. He'd make a few bucks. Of course, Aunt Flo was always after him to get it cut. Just like she use to be after me. He'd always say to her, "Let en bide, let en bide if he wants it like that." He'd always stick up for me. And so then things got switched around and it was his own mop she was pestering him about.

When he strolled into the bedroom where me and Brent was that night, he looked first like he wasn't in a very good mood.

"Grandfather," I said to him, "I was just tellin Brent about the times me and you and Dad was out squiddin." I was hoping that would do something to change the serious look he had on his face.

"Told him about the time you almost put your father overboard?"

I didn't want to be getting into that. "Com'on, you knows that's not right. I didn't almost put en overboard."

"Sure I was there," he said, still not smiling.

"I knows you was. He just lost his balance and fell down in the bottom o' the boat, that was all. I wasn't really use to the motor then. I cut the boat too much when I turned to go back in the cove. Sure I was only nine."

Before I got finished his face broke into a grin. I should a known that. He was only trying to tease me.

"I remembers how your father fell down, flozzo, right on top o' the squid we caught, ass first," he laughed.

He didn't need to remind me. And how the old man got so dirty with me for being careless. Although he let me steer the boat back into the wharf just the same.

"Forget about that time," I said. "We'd always jig a nice many, wouldn't we, Grandfather?"

"Yeah, I guess we would. We'd sell some of it," he said, "and dry a bit. Some of it we'd use for bait. And we'd always bring home so many for your mother to stuff and bake."

"You should remember that good enough, Brent. Sure we'd get home and you'd still be half on the bawl cause you didn't get to go."

"I would not."

"You would so," I said. "And then as soon as ever we'd get inside the porch door, Dad'd shout out to see what was on the go for supper. It'd be after dark probably by the time we got home, and we right gone for some food."

"And it was sure to be something good. God, your mother was able to put on some pot o' soup, I can tell you that."

"Mom'd have people in off the road with their tongues hangin out, wouldn't she?"

"Right down to their bootlaces," Brent added.

"Probably your father would march straight into the kitchen then, rubber boots and all on, and plank whatever squid he had into the kitchen sink," Grandfather said.

"And sometimes, just to tease her, he'd bend down and grab Mom around the legs and hoist her up to the ceiling. That man had some strength in hes arms."

"Him trottin around the kitchen with her thcn. Just for the devilment, that's all he done it for. Your Mother'd have to laugh in spite of herself. All of us laughin then when she'd start, gettin a real kick out of it," Grandfather said.

We all laughed. Him and Brent and me. Just the three of us. Grandfather was the only one now who could remember it all, the times that

went on before. We was able to share things that
nobody else could anymore. And I could see it in
his face that he knew it too.

"Grandfather," I said after a while, "squiddin is
a lot o' fun, idn't it?"

"Yes b'y, it is so."

"We'll have to go at it again."

"Yes, I spose."

"And me too this time," Brent said.

"You and me and Poppy."

"All right," Grandfather said. "All right."

That was all that was said about it. We knew,
though, that there was no such thing as all right.
There couldn't be with me gone in a few weeks to
St. Albert, nowheres close to squidding, or to
Grandfather or Brent. Nowheres close to anything
connected to either one of them.

4

Like I said, in lots of ways it was the rottenest summer I ever had. Most summers are over before you knows it and you're back at school with hardly enough time to stop and think. But that summer dragged on and on.

And then Sunday, the second day of September, there I was at the Irving station on the highway waiting for the bus to come. The three of them came to see me off. The waiting was the part that I couldn't stand. If we could a got there just as the bus pulled in, and me got aboard and went on, it would a been okay. But, of course, Aunt Flo had to make sure we was there in plenty of time. So we ended up waiting for twenty minutes.

Perhaps it wouldn't a been so bad except for Brent. All along he hadn't been saying much. Then with about five minutes before the bus was due to come, there he was off to one side by himself, staring at the road and blinking water out of his eyes. He tried to keep from having to look at me.

I went over to him. I might a known that was going to happen. "Look," I told him, "you're not goin to mind it once I gets gone."

He still wouldn't look at me.

I tried to make a joke of it. "There'll be nobody around to bother ya. You'll be able to do just what you likes."

That was even worse. He never budged, and then when I tried to force him to look at me, he broke away and turned back on.

"Listen, what's there to worry about," I half-yelled. "I'll see ya again before long. You can write and I'll promise to write ya back every time."

"I can't write very good."

Dummy. "Then print, for frig's sake."

"Quit swearin at me!" he yelled. He started in bawling.

"Okay, okay. If you're goin to cry then it's no use even tryin to talk to ya. Com'on, stop it."

That made him slack up a bit. "I told ya before what it was going to be like. And buddy, you better start in gettin use to it. Sure you got Aunt Flo. And Poppy is there. What more do ya want? She's goin to be takin good care of ya."

"It won't be the same."

"Now, it's no good startin that. I didn't want for us to have to split up. You knows that. But right now it's sposed to be the best thing. And I guess we just got to go along with it. But I knows one thing—if you behaves yourself and tries to get

along with Aunt Flo all ya can, then that's going
to be a whole lot better for all of us. But if you
stays like you are here now, with a mouth on ya
all screwed up, then that's going to make it ten
times worse for everybody."

He didn't say anything.

"Now you just remember what I said. And
don't let me hear tell of anything from Aunt Flo
about you being a nuisance to her."

"Ah, keep quiet!"

"I'll keep quiet, but you just remember that."

"You shut up and worry about yourself!"

The bus hauled into the garage and I had to
leave him. I was the only one getting on and I
knew the bus would be stopping only just long
enough for that. The driver took the suitcases and
box I had and stowed them away with the rest of
the luggage.

I let Aunt Flo have her little peck on my cheek.
I figured that wasn't much on my part. But, before
I knew it, she had her arms wrapped around me
and nearly had my chest caved in. Now *she* was
the one half on the bawl.

I shook Grandfather's hand and said good-bye
to him.

"Michael, take care of yourself." I was going
to miss him an awful lot.

And Brent. I didn't know really what to do.
Trying to shake his hand or something would a
seemed too stupid.

"See ya, buddy," I said, and sorta just smiled at him.

"Yeah, see ya." His eyes red and watery.

Then Aunt Flo piped up, just as I turned to go aboard the bus, "Put on plenty o' clothes now. Keep yourself warm." All the people with the windows open and looking out at us.

Cripes, she went and done it again. Leave it to a woman to make a fellow feel like a fool in front of strangers. I took off up the steps. The driver punched my ticket and then I walked straight back without turning the head one way or the other. I planked myself down in the first vacant seat I came to.

I might as well lay this fair and square on the line. Then maybe you'll understand what caused all the racket on the stupid bus.

How old you are is a big deal when you're growing up. That's almost the first bloody thing anybody'll ask about when they meets you, right —how old you are? Well, like I said, I'm fourteen. I turned fourteen not long ago, in May. But I'm still no fantastic size. It's only now that I'm starting to shoot up like a weed and getting hair all over the place. Some fellows my age got into that a good while back and are a nice bit taller than me already. But I don't really care. So what difference do it make?

Well, the darn big difference that it makes is when you starts talking about adults. And the way a good many of them have got of treating you. A lot of adults looks at someone fourteen and right away all they figures is you're out to cause trouble. Now, I'll grant you, some I can think of ain't much better than that. But lots of people thinks they can lump us all together and stick the same label on the whole works of us. And that's bull. Pure bull.

Now, for all the trouble I got into on the bus, it was only because I told him to shut up. All I done was tell this lousy drunk to keep his mouth closed. And don't say he wasn't asking for it, the state he was in.

The seat I sat myself down into was the first empty one I came across. I wasn't particular about where I sat, all I wanted was to get away from Aunt Flo and her preaching about me having to keep warm. After the bus started up I realized then just where I had planked myself—right next to some guy who was plastered drunk. Not hard to see why the seat was empty. Cripes, if I'd a stopped for half a second before I sat down I would've had a big enough whiff of booze to drive me away from it. As it was, when they did get to me, I just about conked out with the fumes. I could see too how the stupid jerk had got himself polluted. In the overnight bag he had stuffed down by his feet was three of those screw-top drink bottles and only one of them had anything left in it. And for sure it wasn't just Coke.

I mightn't a said anything to him atall, if he

had kept quiet and gone to sleep or something. I might a stayed where I was and put up with the smell if he hadn't opened his mouth so quick.

"How's ya gettin on, young fella." He mumbled out the words. His stinking breath blowed across my face, the same time as his hand was bouncing off the top of my knee. He looked at me, his head cocked to one side, with a foolish grin on the face. I shoved his hand away. He straightened up a bit.

"Keep them hands to yourself," I told him. I wasn't going to have the likes of that pawing all over me.

He tried to straighten up more.

"I was only sayin hello to ya, kid. Whas da matter wit ya?"

"Frig off." He might a been queer for all I knew. He stared at me like I had two heads.

"Jesus, yer some touchy."

"Just keep to yourself."

Another whiff of rum and it all came back to me even worse about the accident. That was the kind of drunken no-goods who got people killed. Get some liquor into them and they thinks they can do like they please. They let the likes of that stay on the bus then and bother other people. It made me sick to my stomach.

"How ol are ya, anyway?" he mumbled some more.

I wouldn't answer him.

"How ol are ya?" Louder, like I had to be deaf or something.

"If it was any of your business I'd tell ya," I said in his face. It was then I started to get up outa the seat.

He could see that I was moving. And all of a sudden it got to be a big insult. Just as if he was the best company anyone ever had.

"Whas ya too good to sit by me, are ya? Then, get lost, ya little bastard."

He said the last of it under his breath, but I heard what he said good enough. That was all I was about to take coming from something like that.

"You shut up your lousy mouth! Who the frig do you think you are, anyway? You should be kicked off this bus. You're the one who should be movin, not me."

When I said that, all the people in the seats around whipped their heads up and glued their eyes to us to see what was going on. It shocked a good many of them up off their rear ends. I heard one old crab go "tut-tut-tut." Well, let her tut-tut all she wanted.

"The language! Where do they get it from? Sure he's only a youngster."

That got me all the more spitey. "He's drunk," I told them all. "He's drunk. He can hardly see outa hes two eyes. He stinks o' rum."

They had me figured for someone half crazy, the way I was yelling like that. And only a youngster! That's what they had in their minds.

"Com'on and see for yourself. You wanta sit by en?"

Then this fellow from two seats behind gets up and comes over to me. I spose he figured he was the world's number-one peacemaker or something. Like some big ox, he puts his arm around my shoulders and tries to lead me down to another seat. The jerk.

I broke away from him. "Let go! You don't believe me, do ya? Just look at him. You think that should be allowed on the bus?"

"It's okay. Just leave him alone. He's quiet enough. He's not doing any harm," the ox says. "Come back here, now. There's an empty seat back here." And he tries to lead me away to it.

"Let go, you!"

Not him or any one of them on the stupid bus could a cared less about whether or not what I said was true. All them dummies was interested in was getting me to keep quiet.

Sure I got riled up. But I had a darn good right to get riled up, didn't I?

I'm not that stupid you know. Any fellow fourteen knows what he's talking about when it comes to liquor. I've been around people drinking enough times for that. And I've had plenty myself.

Sure as long as I can remember, Dad would let me have some of whatever it was he was drinking, anytime he ever had it in the house. No big lot, but enough to get a darn good taste of it for sure. And the bunch that I hung around with, every so often we'd get a hold of a half dozen ourselves and share them out. Maybe if it was around Christmas or something and it was easy to get. But we never went at it like some fellows. My son, I've seen fellows a lot younger than me right clean off the head with booze. So don't think I don't know what I'm talking about.

It's like everything else now. Some is sensible about it and some won't stop until they goes right off the deep end. Just like that stupid fellow on the bus.

Pretty soon all that racket was making the bus driver fidgety. He geared the bus down, brought her off the road, and stopped her. He got up out of his seat and marched back to us.

"Now what's all the trouble about?" he said. Loud, too, after he got a good look at how big I was.

"This drunk here should be kicked off the bus," I said. "Look at him, he can't even keep hes head up straight."

The dummy whipped up his head when I said that. He started to mumble. "I wasn't doin a thing until this young punk . . ."

"Look, look, plastered right out of hes mind."

The bus driver looked him over. When he seen the empty bottles in the bag by his feet, he took one up and smelled it.

"I was sittin down next to en and he started pesterin me.

"What did he do?"

"Well, he started breathin alcohol down my throat the minute I sat down next to en. And he was talkin, buggin me the whole time I was there."

"Yeah, how?"

"He put hes hand on my leg." Some jerk up front started to laugh. "Well, he might be queer! What difference do it make anyway what he done? He's drunk, idn't he? You're not sposed to have drunks on the bus, now are ya?"

"No."

"Well, why don't you kick en off?"

"Listen, kid . . ."

"Don't go callin me kid."

"Listen, he's on here now and that's all I can do about it. I'm not going to kick him out on the highway in the middle of nowhere. Besides, he's not bothering anyone now. Just leave him alone and he'll go off to sleep."

See what I mean. Now, if I'd been anybody older he would a up boots and flattened that drunk. All the stupid driver done was take his part.

"Now," he said, "you'll have to find another seat. This is putting us behind schedule. He'll be off the bus in another hour, anyway. You come up front with me. You'll be far enough away from him then."

That didn't satisfy me one bit. But I ended up going. I didn't have much choice. The driver asked one of the people in a front seat if he would move down to the back. On the way up to the front they was all looking at me like I was some kinda troublemaker. They still didn't believe that lousy drunk had started it. They was willing to put the whole blame on me. I spose they figured it was okay to be plastered right outa the mind on a public bus. That was okay. But let some young fellow try to stand up for his rights, that was another story.

I didn't hardly move after I sat down. But I was fuming up inside the whole time. The ones getting off the bus had a last look at me. One dumb clot even said, "I gotta go now for a beer," just as he was walking past me. You knows darn well he said it for me to hear.

Then when it came time for the drunk to get off, the driver had to practically carry him down over the steps. He was too far gone even to notice who I was. Good thing too. Because if he had said anything to me I would a give him a damn good clop across the chops. Don't think I wouldn't've.

PART TWO

5

By the end of two weeks at Uncle Ted's place, I'd seen enough to know exactly what I thought of the family I was in with and of the whole lot they calls St. Albert. I arrived there on a Sunday night. By four o'clock on Monday they had me carted around to everything within five miles that they said was worth seeing. I was beat to a salve by the time they was through trying to make me feel welcome.

And it didn't impress me much what I seen. St. Albert is sposed to be a city—a small one, but they calls it a city just the came. Take a newsprint mill, an airport, shopping malls, two arenas, and together with the holy crowd of houses that are there, then you have a city. All that they figured was something to be proud of. It's okay for them to like it I spose, but to me it wasn't worth much when I thought of the other places I knew that got none of that and looks to me like better places to be living. I mean, things like a Dairy Queen and two Kentucky Fried Chicken joints don't mean shag all to me. The food was okay for a change but other than that it was nothing to kick up a fuss over. Sometimes they gave out free plastic banks. Wow! More thrills than a boatload of rotten fish.

I should try to be fair about the whole thing, I spose. Some of the stuff I liked. The movie theatres. The places to go skating and the swimming pool. Drop these down in the middle of some community with five hundred people, a good harbour, and closed in around with a nice big stretch of woods, then I'd move there tomorrow. But the way it was with me then, I was far from raving about the fact of having to live in St. Albert. But I made a promise that I'd give it a try. And I wasn't about to go back on my word.

The first couple of days Uncle Ted and Aunt Ellen tried hard to make me feel welcome. I'll say that much for them. I'm not blaming them for picking a rotten place to live.

Now the part of the city where they lives couldn't be called half bad, if you're talking about the look of the houses and the size of the land they're on. Only thing is, you got a streetful of them all lined up next to each other. And once you're inside the place, well, if you likes modern houses, then Uncle Ted's would be right up your alley—carpet everywhere, even up one wall, fancy lights all over the place, a chesterfield set that sinks down a mile when you lays your rear end on it, and all kinds of other things that we never had home.

I have to say I thought it was sorta nice when I seen it first. But before long I had a change of mind. I mean, it sounds dumb to say that a place is too nice, but that's what it was. There wasn't not one thing outa place, not one thing anywhere but where it was marked for. A newspaper left on the coffee table was like someone had committed a crime. Either someone had to be reading it, or it had to be in the newspaper rack. If you so much as mentioned the word dust, I daresay you'd get sucked up into the Electrolux feet first.

The kitchen was just as bad. The snazziest-looking cupboards you ever seen. The floor then just like the mirror. You practically had to hold your breath so's you wouldn't dull the shine. I knows it wouldn't be the place now for Dad to a been picking a few turrs or cutting the guts outa some fish. I knows Aunt Ellen wouldn't a had the fit. I can fair see it now.

They put me in the same room with Curtis, their own son. For what reason I don't know because they had another bedroom there with no one in it. Perhaps they wanted to save that one for visitors, or maybe Aunt Ellen didn't want the extra dirt to have to clean up. Maybe, too, they figured I needed the company.

Well, that kind of company, the way he was first, I could a done without. Some guys you could call quiet. But this fellow! My lord, he hardly opened his mouth except when he had to yawn. I didn't know first if he was stuck-up or just too shy to say anything. Some guys gets like that.

If books was anything to go by, then I knew from the first time I went in the room that he was some kinda real brain. He's got more books than any fellow I ever knew. Across one shelf he's got every Hardy Boy book that was ever put out, all in order, right tight to each other. And below them, there is about ten times as many other books. Science fiction, a lot of it. See, I wouldn't be able to spend my time at that. Not science fiction. And neither do I go much on Joe and Frank and the boys. Hand me over some books that got to do with animals or cars, or clues me in on something else I wants to find out, then I'm okay. But not any of those dumb detective books. I'd hardly be able to crack the cover to get to the first page.

He does have one set of books that caught my eye. There's a set there on the mammals in North America. Now that was more along my line.

I was in there firking around through his books to see all what he had, when in he came that first time and seen me.

"Got either copy of *Playboy*?" I said to him for a laugh.

He didn't answer me. All he done was put on this little smile.

"None under your mattress?" I was only trying

to be friendly. I only said it for something to say.

"No," he said, like he didn't take it for a joke atall. He sat down at his desk and this time never so much as looked at me.

Well, I thought, this is something now. A fine way to start off. It wasn't as if we'd never seen each other before. This was the first time we'd been together in the room we was sposed to be sharing, that was all. And if a fellow can't look at a pile of someone else's books, what the hell can he do.

I sat down on the bed that Aunt Ellen said was mine. He never even turned his head away from his book. Talk about your friendly relations. It was bugging me, that was. It was just as well to get to the bottom of it right away.

"I can't do much about it," I told him. "This is where your mother put me. You want me to go and ask her if I can move somewhere else? Is that what you wants? If it is, then I'll do it right now and get it over with."

"No, you haven't got to do that," he said.

That surprised me—how quick the answer came outa him. Made me think he was almost afraid of what might happen if I did.

I left it at that. I took my suitcase, opened it up on the bed, and started rooting around. Then for the first time without being asked, he said something. That idea of going to his mother must a done something to loosen him up.

"You can put your clothes over there. That

bureau is empty. And there's plenty of room in the closet for anything you want to hang up."

It was something, but it really wasn't much of a change. What he did say after that was pretty much forced outa him. Whether he was shy or mad at me being there, or whatever it was that made him not want to talk, all of it was a real pain in the neck. The first couple of days was enough to drive anyone foolish. You should a seen us. It's a laugh when I thinks back on it now. He might a said ten words about his stupid stamp collection and I'd say "yeah" and try to show I was interested. Then maybe I'd go on for ten minutes about the .22 I got last Christmas and at the end of it all he might nod his head. If I was lucky. By the second night I'm sure we was both wishing there was a six-foot brick wall up between us.

See, part of it was we hardly had a darn thing in common. Most of the stuff he grew up interested in, I couldn't a cared less about. And the other way around. I just couldn't figure it out how we was ever going to stick it living in the same room together.

Finally what did make matters better between me and Curtis was school. See, what I figured too was that he thought I was dumb. That because I didn't know much about any of the stuff he was interested in, and him being something of a brain in school, then he thought there wasn't much more than sawdust between my ears. After I got his little mind straightened out on that one, then we got along a hundred percent better.

Before I made the move to St. Albert, I'd gone to the same school all my life. There was just the one school for Marten and the couple of other places near to it. The school was split up into two parts—kindergarten to grade six on one side and the high school on the other, with a gym and resource centre between them. But it was all under the one roof. There was maybe three hundred students altogether.

When I moved I was ready to start grade nine. For the first few days in the new school I was in pretty slack shape about knowing where to go. Cripes, you could a fitted the school I went to before into what this place had for a gym. There was way more of everything you could name— students, teachers, equipment, secretaries, everything. It was like the Confederation Building compared to what I was use to. And it only had three grades in it. Only students in seven, eight, and nine. It took a bit of catching on for me to get myself organized.

The first thing I got thrown at me was a placement test. That was sposed to tell them what class they was going to put me in—A, B, C, D, or E. Where I came from, grade nine was grade nine, no more to it than that. Now I was going to be crowned with a letter too. All depending, of course, on how smart or how stupid the test showed I was.

I had one thing going for me. I wasn't nervous about writing the test. Mr. Graham, the guidance counsellor, had me there in a booth in his office, but I wasn't either bit on edge. That's one thing about me. I don't get nervous writing tests. Some fellows'll tense right up, like they've been hauled up before a firing squad. Me, I writes what I can as best I can, and that's it. I stops there.

There was a few things on the test I never had much of a clue about. I skipped over them. I guess that's what put me in the B class for most of the subjects I was going to take. They had me down for math and science out with the A crowd. I was always good at them. Math I could whip off no sweat. I never seen much use for a lot of it, but there was no sweat getting it done. And science. I guess they looked pretty hard at what I had down on the science part of the paper. One question said, "Name five classes of vertebrates and write a description of each one." I filled out four pages. That must a made someone's eyes pop open.

That's how me and Curtis got together in school —for those two subjects. Of course, he was in the A class all the way.

School is a funny thing. Sometimes I got the best kinda interest in it. More times I wish I could chuck it all up and not see the sight of a school book no more. I always did get pretty good marks. Not because I studied a real lot, but mainly because I paid attention in class and always got my homework done on time. When I looks back to when I ever made a balls of it on a test, it was usually in some subject where I was bored to death with the teacher.

Science was always my best subject. For science, me and Curtis had this Mr. Marshall. He was half decent, I spose. But the best part of it was the science lab we had the classes in. The whole back of one wall had shelves full of biology material. That was the first place I headed for when I went in through the door. They must a had twenty-five or more different animal skeletons mounted and put on the shelves. I've seen parts of skeletons in the woods lots of times, or when someone throwed away the carcass of a mink or something they skinned and it rotted, but I never did see them cleaned and mounted like they had them there. And live rabbits and guinea pigs and mice. They even had a snake crawling around in a glass cage. That was the first one I ever seen alive, because there aren't any wild in Newfoundland. Not even any grass snakes.

Our class was new to Mr. Marshall, so he didn't know any more about any one of us than he did about the others. I was glad of that. That first day, after he marked the attendance sheet and stuff, we got into talking about what we would be doing during the year. We had a textbook we would be using a lot. But he said he was "open to suggestions" for other topics.

"The female body" says one wiseguy. Then some girl, not going to be outdone, snaps back with "the male body." Marshall cuts them off right there. And after a coupla minutes when nobody suggests anything he calls reasonable, I comes up with something I've had in mind all along—"animal life in the Atlantic." That gets a better reaction from him.

"For any particular reason?" he asks.

And so I tells him that since we're living on an island and surrounded by all that salt water and since fishing has always been so important to us, why not spend time learning something more about that, instead of talking about a lot of other stuff we've never even seen. He sorta picked up from there, and we got to discussing all kinds of different animals in the oceans. Well, it turned out I knew a lot more than anybody else in the class about the animal species in the North Atlantic. The different species of fish, the whales and the seals, all that. A good bit of it I'd seen for myself, like when I've been out jigging cod and come across porpoises jumping around. I didn't want to start off the year like I was a real brain or something, so I shut up then and didn't say no more.

I think that little discussion I had with Marshall set Curtis back a few notches. There was a lot more in my head than he thought. Everything people knows don't come from books, like he figured. I picked up a lot of that just from living near the salt water all my life and listening to Grandfather and some others, and those who've been out to the seal hunts.

Curtis started to look at me different after that and we got on a whole lot better. There was still a good many things about him that I didn't have much use for, and probably if we had never been forced together, we would never even got to know each other atall. But when he found out that I wasn't a dumb jerk like he had in his mind first, then we started in at least talking sensible to each other. That was a big improvement right there.

6

I wasn't smart enough to see it at the time, but my first few days at their house must a been real torture for not only Curtis, but for everybody there. The only difference was, the others done a better job of covering it up. Uncle Ted and Aunt Ellen did spend a lot of their time trying to be nice to me, and it looked first like they really meant it. But now I can see that it was something they done only because they figured they had to. Really they didn't too much like the idea that they was being forced to make someone else a part of their life. They had their ways of doing things and I had mine. I certainly didn't expect them to change to suit me, for the same reason that they couldn't expect me to suddenly be someone I wasn't all along.

I didn't know a hell of a lot about them before I came. That was one of the problems. Dad never got along very good with them, I knew that, although Mom would never let him talk to us about why. I guess that should a told me something right there. Then, as the days went by, I started to find out more and more of the reasons for it. A good many more than I ever expected.

There's four in their family altogether. The other one is Marie, Curtis' older sister. Marie has all the interesting parts that goes together to make up a sixteen-year-old female. Only problem is—she's got too much of most of them. A nice kind word would a been overweight. Curtis called her flabby. She wouldn't give him so much as the time of day. Me either, for that matter. She dumped me right away into the category of boys who are interested in girls but who are not old enough yet to be of any interest to her. I let it stay like that.

I never really seen that much of her anyway. Although I heard enough, that was one thing for sure. She was a telephone freak if there ever was one. I wouldn't doubt but she had a red ring around her ear, she used it that much. The only times her eardrums ever got a rest must a been when she was asleep.

I spose after the first while of having me in the house, all of them started to ease off a bit on the front they had rigged up. Their true selves started to show through. After all the novelty of me being there rubbed off, they started to get back to the way they must a been before I came.

I mean, I'm no stranger to arguments. Me and Mom and Dad had our fights the same as people in any family. Sometimes they was only in fun.

Other times, I'd get vicious about something and slam a few doors. But whoever was right, it was all forgot about afterwards.

The only reason the first argument I heard in the house between Uncle Ted and Marie got me upset was because of the way he yelled at her. See, I wasn't sposed to have heard it. It was in the middle of the second week I was there, about ten-thirty in the night and I was sposed to be gone to bed like Curtis. But I wasn't. I was in the kitchen getting something to drink. Uncle Ted figured we was both in the room with the door closed.

"This is not enough to get me through the week." That was the first words I heard. My ears perked up. The fight was over money. It wasn't the last one I was to hear about that.

"Well, that's all you're getting," Uncle Ted said. Sounded to me like he wasn't about to change his mind.

"It's not enough," Marie said. I could barely hear her voice.

"Just tell me what you need more than that for. You're not running the British Navy for God's sake." No trouble to hear him, though.

"For everything."

"Everything! That's some answer I know. Okay, you buy everything you can till the money runs out. Then all you got to do is stop." He started to laugh.

"Dad, I need to buy some new clothes for school. School just opened and I haven't bought one thing."

"Your mother gave you some money for clothes last week."

"It wasn't enough."

"Christ, Marie, I'm not made of money!" he yelled. It was the first time I heard him swear.

"Well, were not exactly poverty stricken."

"Listen, my lady, you've got all you're going to get and that's that. Take it and don't ask for any more. I don't want to hear another word about it. Every week it's the same goddamn thing. I'll be jesus glad when you can earn some money of your own! Then you might see it's not so easy to come by."

The swear words, when he spitted them out of him, was almost enough to curl up my guts. Not the words, that was nothing. I was use to that. But the way he said them. People swears in different ways. Dad use to swear and he hardly had a clue he was saying it. But the way the same words came out of Uncle Ted, it was like a set of teeth tearing into her.

Marie took off running down the hall, probably crying. I couldn't tell. It was then I got stunned even worse than before. I heard someone in the living room say to him, "Ted, try not to be so hard on her." It was Aunt Ellen. All that time she was in the room with them and she'd never said a word.

"Ellen," he told her, in just about the same voice he used on Marie, "don't poke your nose into this! I handle the money. You stay out of it."

Stunned again. I never heard a man speak like that before to his wife and mean it, the way Uncle Ted sounded like he did. Maybe I was just dumb when it came to the way other parents talked to each other. I laid down the empty tumbler fast on the table and snuck out into the hall and tried not to make a sound the whole way down to the room. I got inside and closed the door quietly behind me.

That night, lying there on the bed, I had a lot to think about. I wasn't sure what to make of it. I mean, perhaps Marie did waste loads of money. I didn't know. Even if she did, that wasn't much of a way to talk to her. It wasn't even a sensible argument. All it was was someone laying down the law. And what he said to Aunt Ellen. Sure you wouldn't talk to your dog like that. I knows Mom wouldn't a hauled off and clobbered anybody who said that to her. No, it's a laugh she wouldn't've. I'd be half scared to blink my eyes, afraid I'd miss it.

As the next few weeks went by, Uncle Ted started to paint a pretty clear picture of the way he really was. And it was a picture that I wasn't very fussy about, that's for sure. If I'd a known about it before I left to come, they wouldn't a dragged me from Marten, no not with a dozen teams of wild horses. It must a been some strain on him to be half decent the way he was first when I came, that's all I can say. Going by what he was after, I would a give him a cartload of trophies for the show he put on.

Once he got himself into the right gear, it all boiled down to this—the way he wanted things in the house was the way they had to be done. That was it. No questions asked unless you wanted a bloody big fight on your hands. It was up to him when we had supper, who done the dishes. He decided what channel was on the colour T.V., what time everyone was expected to be in bed, what time everyone was awake in the morning. Cripes, it got so after a while I didn't know whether or not I should try going to the bathroom to take a leak without first getting his okay.

He never said much straight out to me about what I was expected to do. Good thing for him that he didn't. It was just taken for granted that I would follow along like everyone else. I did too, for awhile, because when you're asked into someone else's house you don't go picking fights right away with the one who owns the place. It's only when things gets too much outa hand. Then you got to draw the line.

See, it wasn't just the arguments and the big-boss bit I didn't like. It was his whole way of looking at things that got on my nerves after a spell. After the first few days, I hardly ever seen him crack a smile, not what you could call a honest-to-goodness smile. When he did laugh, it was usually at someone else, the way they done things. He might a made out he was in a good mood sometimes, but just let anyone do one little thing he didn't like and see how long he'd stay that way. Worst of all was how he always snapped back at people when they said anything against him. Worse than a huskie dog that hadn't been fed.

I kept quiet about it all, kept what I thought to myself. I was in a different position than what Marie and Curtis was. I hadn't gone through all my life living with him like they'd done. And he never talked to me the way he did to them. So I wasn't about to start a racket. Not that I didn't have a good mind to sometimes. I had that much hopping around on my tongue I had to force my mouth shut to keep it all in.

It would a been different altogether if I had been Curtis. I just didn't understand that fellow. He took it all like he was a dummy. If he didn't think his old man was right about something, say when he'd get a big goin-over for stupid little things like breaking a glass, he might say that he didn't try to do it and leave it at that. Or say it was a week night and not even nine-thirty and too early to go to bed, he might tell his father that he didn't really want to and then there would be no more said about it. After another five minutes he'd go to the room and start getting undressed. I mean, he wasn't a kid anymore. He was the same age I was. It wasn't like he was five years old and should a been stuck in bed whether he liked it or not.

Sure I got madder than he did himself about the way he got told what to do all the time. He had his books and it almost looked to me like that was all he wanted. Sometimes he never even got to enjoy them. Every school night about ten-thirty there'd be a march past the door by the old man to make sure there was no lights still on in the room. Then he'd double back, open the door fast and stick his head in. Like we was prisoners in a jail cell or some bloody thing.

Could you understand something like that? I couldn't. To me it was all a pile of bull. The man wasn't a father if he was forever a pain in the arse. It's one thing to keep order around the house, but it's something else again when a fellow can't have a minute's peace because someone is always on his back.

I had it in my mind a good many times to say that to Curtis. In the nighttime, before I'd be asleep, I'd try to come up with something to say to him a little less mean, that maybe wouldn't hurt his feelings. I tried hard, but I could never figure out anything that was nice enough and still told the truth.

After a time, it was that too that brought me and Curtis together, into being better friends. I found out that neither one of us had much use for that old man of his.

*   *   *

I knows what some of you are thinking. That just because my own father was dead, I'd never find anything to like in any father that wasn't the way he was. Well, that's not true atall. You're probably thinking too that up to then I always got my own way about everything and now I was mad because that wasn't the way it was anymore. Well, you're wrong. I wasn't brought up a spoiled brat. I got told off a good many times and made to do things I didn't much like. But Mom and Dad always tried to be fair about everything, that's the difference. So if that's the way you're thinking, then you can just get it outa your head right now.

Another reason I was bugged was because the way the old man went about things rubbed off on everybody else in the house. They all walked around looking like they was so bloody miserable most of the time. If they smiled at all their faces probably would a cracked in two pieces. They might a had ten times more stuff in their house than we ever had, but they was no better off for it. You'd think they never had a cent to their names, the way they went around forever being crabby to each other. Maybe the old man's business was doing rotten or something, I didn't know. He sold cars. I was down to his showroom once or twice, but he never said anything about it for me to hear.

I thought too, first when I came, that maybe Aunt Ellen would a been different than she was.

I mean, she was good enough to me with regards to food and money and things like that. I had no reason to complain there. And I made sure that every now and then I'd tell her how much I liked what she cooked. She got right off on the compliments, because I don't figure she ever had very many of them.

But still for all she looked to be pretty much in the dumps most of the time. She never said anything about it. She never said all that much, period. I guess he would a put a stop to that. I'd like to've known how in the world she ever got mixed up with someone like him in the first place.

One of the only things I ever seen her get a real kick out of was the story that comes on T.V. in the afternoon. About four-thirty every day, there she'd be, mind stuck to the set, tea in one hand, a cigarette in the other. Her right caught up in every word that was being said. She'd hardly notice me when I'd come into the room. She wouldn't miss not a second of it. Anything she had to do in the kitchen, she'd rush in and do it during the commercials. I didn't understand what she seen in it, myself. How anyone could spend so much time watching the same people in some kind of misery with each other every single day was beyond me. But I spose she got something out of it, whatever it was.

7

The way everything was being done in the house, it all took some getting use to. As much as I could, I kept to myself when I was there. I spent most of my time in the bedroom or downstairs in the rec room.

And I didn't come to like school near as good as I liked it in Marten, even though the school in St. Albert was bigger and had a lot more. I guess it was because in Marten I knew everybody.

Usually I don't find it hard to make friends. I turns after Dad when it comes to that, because he'd go up to anyone atall, whether he knew them or not, and have the biggest kinda chat. I'm usually something the same way. And I was stupid enough to think that it would work in that school too. That it was just a matter of starting up a conversation and everybody would be friendly. Well, I was dead wrong there.

On the second morning, there I was hanging around this bunch of fellows in the corridor during recess, saying a few things to them. All of a sudden they started in looking at me like I was a real fool, like I was some kinda nut to be talking to them when they didn't know me. The friggers, they kept on laughing at me even after I moved away.

I had to spend the rest of recess then walking around the corridors, trying not to look like I never had anyone to talk to. I had one eye out for Curtis, but I didn't come across him anywhere. Then, just as the bell went, I met up with this fellow who seemed to be a bit more civilized.

"Don't mind those other guys," he said to me. "They're a real bunch of jerks." He must a seen what happened. He was on his way to the same class I was, but we didn't get much of a chance to speak to each other because as soon as we went in the classroom the teacher came in and started talking. Not even a chance to find out buddy's name.

It was history class. The teacher got into it right away about the Micmacs and the Beothucks. He switched on full force. After a while, though, what he was saying all got to be pretty interesting. I thought a lot about the Beothucks before, ever since we studied a poem about them once. I mean, it was a rotten thing what happened to them. Here they was, this group of Indians in Newfoundland before any white fellow ever set foot on the place, and they all died or got killed off, and for no reason except that the settlers figured it was no great loss to anyone if they was dead. I heard

Grandfather say he heard tell that when the Beothucks lived around home, someone came once
and slaughtered fourteen of them the one time. It's
hard to believe, that is. But I knows for a fact
myself that they lived near home, because some
of us found flints and there've been cooking
places found down near Birchy Cove.

I had a good mind to tell the teacher all that. If
I was back in my old school I would've. Not
hesitated a bit. But instead I got my mind back to
just listening to him. He started reading from
these old books where different travellers had
mentioned the Beothucks and how they lived. I
was figuring that I'd have no worries about my
history mark if that was the kind of stuff we
would be doing.

Then Mr. Harris, that was his name, started in
asking questions. You can always tell who's going
to get asked first. It's the same way with any
teacher—the person that shows either sign of not
paying attention. One of the fellows over by the
window was his first victim. The fellow didn't
have a clue what he was talking about. He didn't
even have the sense to fake an answer. All the
teacher asked him was how he thought the
Beothucks would be treated if there was some
still alive today. I mean, any dummy could give
an opinion. The fellow just shook his head.

That's the way it always happens. The teacher
asks a couple that he thinks won't have an answer,
bawls them out and gives a little lecture about

not paying attention, then goes on to someone who looks like they might know something.

After about five minutes he got around to me. First I wasn't sure if I should say much because I was in this class where I didn't know anyone. And some of them jerks who'd been in the corridor was in the class too. What the hell, I thought, I don't give a darn about them.

I told the teacher what he wanted to know about where the last of the Beothucks died, and when and how. I probably should a stopped there. But before I knew it *I* was asking *him* questions. One thing got around to another, and in a few minutes I was telling him about all the stuff we found. Flints that we was sure must a been used by the Beothucks and how we almost went so far as to dig up what we thought was a grave. Only someone from the university in St. John's came out and stopped us.

The teacher was really interested in what I was saying and so was most of the others in the class. But I could see two or three of the jerks laughing to each other. The hell with them.

The bell rang and Mr. Harris said we would carry on the discussion the next day and how interesting it was and all that. I got up to leave when the fellow who was talking to me before came over and started chatting away again and asking me questions. Like where I was from and that. I told him and we talked back and forth all the way to the next class. Gerard was his name.

Gerard was to become the best friend I would ever make in that school.

The class after history was English. In a different room, but with all the same students. The two of us sat down and kept on talking, waiting for the teacher to come in. I wasn't paying much heed to the others, but just before the English teacher came through the door, I heard this voice from the back of the room.

"Back home in Marten, we was always right good at suckin up to teachers."

I whipped my head around to see who said it. One of those friggin dummies was mocking what I'd said to Mr. Harris in the other class. There was no way to telling who it was—I seen three or four of them who laughed at me in the corridor all snickering away. Cripes, I was vicious! But by then the teacher was stood up there in front of the class ready to start and I couldn't say a god-blessed thing. And what pissed me off even more was the fact that I had turned red in the face. Like they had embarrassed me. It wasn't that atall. I was just too bloody mad to be any other colour.

It's hard to say what I would a done if the teacher hadn't come in when he did. I daresay I would a pitched right into the whole damn lot of them. Give them a friggin good piece of my fist they didn't plan on.

All the way through English class I couldn't keep my mind atall on what I was sposed to be doing. It was an interest questionnaire or some stupid thing.

Making fun like that gets me savage—making fun of people because of the way they talks and because I asked Harris a few lousy questions. Everyone around home talks like I do. What bloody odds do it make anyway, as long as people understands what you got to say?

And him, whoever he was, saying that I was sucking up to the teacher. The stupid jerk. I wished to God I had it by the scruff of the neck. He wouldn't a said it more than once. No, by frig, he wouldn't've.

Gerard slipped a note across to me. I unfolded the bit of paper and read it. The note said, "It was either George Simmons, Gene Morris, or Lewis Kentson. They're the biggest——in school. Take it from me—forget them. It'll only get you in worse trouble."

He didn't fill in the blank in case the teacher ever got hold of the note. But I had no trouble filling it in in my mind. I sent back the very same slip of paper with two more words scrawled across the bottom of it—"Like hell." Boy, was I ever mad.

By the time the bell rang for the end of class, I had cooled down a bit from what I was first. The English teacher was still collecting up his papers when I went out the door and set up watch for them in the corridor. Gerard came up by me, trying to talk me outa saying anything to them. He was wasting his breath.

The three dummies came out together, laughing and carrying on like a bunch of goons. When they came near where I was standing I stepped out straight in front of them.

"Which one of you jerks made fun of me in there?" I said.

For a second they didn't realize what was going on. They didn't figure me for one who would come back at them.

"What's your problem?" one said.

"You heard me. Which one of you was it or haven't you got the guts to say?"

"This baywop's got a problem with his words," one said to the others, laughing like it was all a big joke. "He's going to have to learn to speak better if he's going to suck up to the English teacher."

"Yeah, or he might as well stay 'back home in Marten' where he belongs."

"You blood-of-a-bitch!" I fired down my books and grabbed into the last fellow who spoke. He wasn't expecting it. I grabbed his shirt with my two hands and hauled it tight around his lousy throat. He must a been two inches taller than me.

It turned out that the guy was Kentson. I gave him a darn good shove and sent him flying back against one of the lockers. His books went everywhere. I would a had the shit knocked outa him too if the other two goons hadn't dragged me clear. I was spittin fire. I was just about free from them and ready to plow right into the other jerk again, when the English teacher came out and saw us.

"What's going on here?" he yelled.

"Nothing, sir," Gerard said, trying to smooth it over. "Just a little disagreement."

"Disagreement! Yes, it sure looks like a *little* disagreement. You fellows want to get sent to the principal's office? You know this is only the second day of school? Get to your classes right now, all of you. If I see that again, I'll have you put on detention for a month."

Gerard helped me collect up my books. The others took off down the corridor while the teacher stood up watching me.

That was the way it ended. What a rip off! I would a had him pounded good if I'd a had half a chance. Instead it was all over and nothing much done. Although there was one thing for sure—they wouldn't be so darn slick the next time to open their mouths. I knew that for a fact.

By the next day it was all over the school about a new fellow getting into a scrape with Kentson and about just how it started. I kept getting stares from one corridor to the other. People I never even seen before started coming up to me and talking and saying that Kentson needed something like that a long time ago, because "he's always shooting off his big mouth."

I came to find out that a good many of them was Gerard's friends. The ones everybody else called "the bus crowd"—those that didn't live right in St. Albert, but came in every day on bus from a place called Simon's Bay, eight miles outside. The bus crowd hung around a lot together in the one group. In fact, the whole school was made up of groups that stuck to theirselves. The ones who figured they was the big shots was Kentson and that bunch—the stuck-up jerks I tried to talk to before I had either clue as to what I was doing. If you went by them, the bus crowd was sposed to be the bottom of the barrel.

It was almost like I got to be adopted as a hero for the way I stood up to Kentson so quick. I didn't know what to make of it. But it's no good saying that I didn't enjoy it, cause I did.

Gerard turned out to be the best of the lot. The others was nice enough, but Gerard and me got along like we'd been buddies all our lives. When we met together before school and between classes we spent the time talking about fishing and all the other things I knew most about. Where he came from was a lot like Marten. A little bit bigger maybe, but the fellows done all the same kinds of things.

8

When it came to the house, there I was fitting in like two left hands in a right-handed mitt. The only one I had much time for anymore was Curtis.

Me and Curtis got off on the wrong foot, but after the first few days we was managing it pretty good. When I went home that Wednesday after getting into it with Kentson, he didn't say anything about what happened. In fact, it was almost two weeks later, after we'd started to get along better with each other, that he brought it up. Up till then, it was mostly me who got underway any of the talks we had. He had just that minute crawled into bed when he propped himself up on one elbow and looked across the room at me. Dead serious.

"Too bad you didn't beat the piss outa that Kentson while you were at it," he said.

I almost thought I should run off to the bathroom, get a box of Q-tips and clean out my ears. That? Coming from Curtis?

"Why, what's he done now?" I said.

"Nothing new. Just that he's forever got his tongue going. He thinks there's no one like himself."

"How'd you get to know en?"

"He used to be in my class last year," Curtis said. "But his marks were so bad that this year they dropped him down to all B classes. Someone told me that his father was in to see the principal about it and kicked up the biggest kind of stink trying to get him put back in A. He never got moved back, though."

"Yeah, I guess we're stuck with him."

"I'm just glad he's not in my class anymore."

"Did he ever do anything to ya?"

"No."

It wasn't a very convincing "no." It was a "no" that came across more like a "yes."

"Had hes mouth goin about something I bet. What was it?"

"Ah, his mouth was always goin about something. He use to stick names on me. That was most of it."

"Did you have a crack at en or what?"

"I thought about it a lot," he said, trying to sound brave. The way he said it, I could just picture what took place.

"That's your problem," I told him. "You don't stand up for your rights."

He never said anything.

"What, you afraid you'll get your face beat in? Sure he's not much bigger than you."

Of course there was more muscle on a turnip top. But that shouldn't a stopped him from trying, from standing up to somebody when he had good reason to. I mean, fighting never done anybody much good when you sizes it up, but there comes a point where you got to stick up for who you are, whether it means a racket or not. But I guess if I had as much chance as Curtis did of coming out on the winning end of a fight, then I'd be scared stiff too.

I tried to make him see that the type Kentson was, he only picked on someone he figured wouldn't fight back anyway. I was telling him this when all of a sudden we heard the army sergeant outside. That was the new name I had stuck on him. Just as I stretched my arm up to switch off the lamp, the door opened and in he walked.

"Curtis," he said, "it's time you were asleep. Cut out your talking now and get some shut-eye. Off with the light. Morning comes early, you know." Then, with the room dark, he goes out and closes the door.

Morning comes early! Wow, the man was brilliant!

After the troop inspection was over, I just had to say something to Curtis about it. I couldn't hold it in anymore.

"Curtis, don't that get on your nerves?"

"What?"

"The dumb march past the door every night.

Cripes, you wouldn't know but we was in the army or something."

Curtis never said anything right away. Then, after about a minute of me wondering whether or not I should a said what I did, he half-whispered, "Sometimes I feel like telling him off. He bugs me."

I didn't know how far I should go with that. After all, it was his father we was talking about now, not some fellow at school. But there wasn't any easy way around it if I was going to tell him what I really thought.

"Sure he treats you like some two-year-old."

"I know."

"Well, why don't you say something to him about it?"

When he didn't answer, I said, "Well, why not?"

"Because he'd only get mad and fly off the handle, that's why."

"Sure, what odds? You wouldn't be any worse off than you are now."

"That's what you think. You don't know what he's like."

"I've heard the arguments."

"That's nothing."

"Whata ya mean, nothing?"

He hesitated for a while. Finally, after a little more coaxing, I got it outa him.

"One time last year he got so mad he fired dinner right across the kitchen while we were at the table. Mom got hit with a piece of glass that cut her face open."

"Frig off."

"No, that's the truth. And he's done a lot worse than that too."

"Like what?"

"Like beat me with a leather belt when I was small till it left black and blue marks."

"Bullshit."

"Wanta make a bet."

Ah, I couldn't really believe that a father would do something like that to his own son. I never ever knew anybody before who told me a story like that and expected me to believe it.

Maybe he *was* telling the truth. If he was, then there was no trouble to see why he would be afraid of his old man.

"Would he try anything like that now?"

"I wouldn't put it past him. It was a long time ago he did anything as bad as that. But I wouldn't cross him up."

"But you can't go on livin like you're scared to death of him."

"Well, just what would you do?"

That stopped me pretty fast, I'll admit. It was a good question. Just what would I do? I wouldn't be in his family to start off with. That much I knew. Then I guess if I was born there like he was . . . well, I did know that I'd stand up to him more than Curtis was doing. Whatever happened to me.

* * *

The talk we had that night done a lot to get the air cleared up. It put a lot of things out in the open and we could discuss them knowing pretty well how the other guy would take it. I wouldn't go so far as to say I liked having to live in St. Albert any better, but at least after that there was one person in the house who I knew I could bang around the truth with. After a while it got so that I could even crack a few jokes and get a good laugh from him. Some of the jokes mightn't a been the cleanest. I don't know where I picked them up. To be honest, I doubt if half the time he knew what I was talking about. But he was willing to laugh and that was the main thing.

I even got into taking up some of his habits. Every night I'd spend a good hour or so reading. I started with the mammal books, hoping that with so much each night I could read my way through them all.

The weekends came to be the worst part of it. Before, I use to be that anxious for the weekends to come that I could barely wait for the last bell to go on Friday. Now it was different. I was glad enough that school was over for the week. No matter how good it was, you had to be glad of that. But there was no real excitement to it when you knew that you'd be spending most of the next two days bored sick. I wasn't on any hockey team or volleyball team or anything, so once I'd been to the arena skating or down to the pool for a swim, then I'd be left with shag all to do during the daytime. Except maybe hang around one of the shopping malls. And who wants to be at that all the time.

The season it was had a lot to do with it. The fall of the year back home meant a lot of other things to me. I use to be in the woods a lot then, after rabbits. That was just about my favorite time of the whole twelve months.

I'd tell Curtis all about what I use to be at in the fall. He might agree with me on how good it was, but I could see he was only doing it to be nice. He didn't know no more about it now than the leg of the chair he was sitting on. But I couldn't get mad at him for that. He didn't grow up spending time in the woods. He wasn't that lucky.

We went to a scattered movie. When we could find one, that is, which didn't have a stupid R or X after the title. And they was few and far between. There wasn't a prayer, not a prayer, of getting in to see those kind by ourselves. As if they could show me something I didn't already know. Half the time all that was left was cartoons, or something else just as bad.

When we went out on weekend nights, usually it was only just to hang around Kelly's drugstore down at the end of the street. Some of Curtis' friends might be there. That didn't automatically make them my friends. And what some of them stood around and gabbed about anyway was enough to drive you crazy. I mean, who wants to be talking about homework on a Saturday night. I wish I could a said I had better things to do with my time, but I didn't.

Sometimes we didn't go out at all. Ended up staying home and watching T.V. That wouldn't a been so bad if the army sergeant hadn't been there to jump down someone's throat at the first bit of noise he didn't like. It got so that most times I'd go downstairs and watch the black and white set rather than stay in the living room where the colour one was and have to listen to him.

Sometimes we was lucky enough to strike a night when he was gone. And better still, some nights the both of them would skin out to the club somewhere and Marie'd be gone, and we'd be left home with the house to ourselves.

This one night that happened and I was bored sick all day anyway, so I got Curtis on the go to make a trip down to Kelly's and invite some people he knew from school back up to the house. I knew that if I left everything up to him, all that would get asked would be his computer-mind friends, so I made sure that some others got in on it too. Some girls. I didn't know any of them, but that was nothing. As long as they wasn't stuck-up, that was all that mattered.

I spose I shouldn't a gone and done it, talked Curtis into letting all those people into the house. He didn't go much on it. What he had on his mind was the mess they might make. But I made good and sure no boots or shoes got past the porch.

There must a been twenty-five people in the house by the time the last ones came through the door.

What they would a done was sit around all night talking and watching the hockey game on T.V. if I hadn't tried to liven things up a bit. I got Curtis to search out Marie's bedroom until he came up with some records. The fellow was mindless when it came to having a good time. I told him not to worry, they'd be all gone by the time his parents got back. Cripes, he wouldn't relax for a minute. All he kept doing was to go around saying to people, "Don't spill anything on the carpet, don't spill anything on the carpet." Like that was all there was to think about.

Inside half an hour I had the whole place organized perfect. So many was in the kitchen making pizza, a couple was sent off down to the store to get some drinks, I had the T.V. off and the stereo on and the place moving like a teenage dance at the Legion on a Friday night. Well, not that much. There was a few stiff-necks who wouldn't get their arses up off the chesterfield. But as for the rest of them, old man, after the first few times, I couldn't put the records on the stereo fast enough. And the faster the music, the better they liked it. I had all I could do to find time to eat.

By eleven o'clock the party was top high. This Dolores someone or other was putting the makes on Curtis. Whata laugh! He might a had some fun out of it too if he hadn't been so darn worried about everything. Every five minutes he'd be looking at his watch.

Then, between one of the songs, we heard the front door open. It was like a ton of concrete came smashing down on him. Every bit of noise disappeared.

Marie trotted in, with a look on her face like she figured for sure she must be in the wrong house. You could hear all the breaths going out the one time. Only Marie, thank God. Curtis' heart took a hundred and eighty degree turn and went back down out of his throat.

He figured for sure we'd better call it quits then. I had to agree with him. So almost as fast as they came in, we paraded them all out again. One false alarm like that would be all we'd be lucky enough to get. So out they all went.

Then we had the job. How to get things back in shape. First we gave Marie a warning to keep her trap shut about what she'd seen. She wasn't even sposed to be home yet. We said it in a nice sorta way, so that perhaps she'd think about helping us with the dishes. No dice, especially when she found out we'd been using her records.

So it was all up to us to get the place spotless again. Curtis on the dishes in the kitchen. Me going like mad with the vacuum cleaner in overdrive. It took a lot of work and we was beat to a pulp by the time we got it all done, but inside forty-five minutes she was looking like new again. All except for this one spot of tomato sauce on the carpet. I rubbed it and rubbed it with a wet cloth till my arm was sore. Then I put the end of the coffee table over it.

We was in bed having the biggest kinda laugh about these two girls Dolores and Daphne when Curtis' parents got home. It must a been one o'clock before they came.

"See, Curtis, you dummy, I told you." Not mad at him really, because it was a good time while it lasted. In fact, thinking about it, it was the only real bit of fun I ever had in that house.

9

That party made me another few friends in St. Albert. They all kept asking when was there going to be another one. But the ones I got along with best at school was still the bus crowd. When October came, Gerard started bugging me to come out to Simon's Bay and stay at his place for a weekend. It would be a real chance to get out and spend some time in the woods like I'd been itching to do all along. The only thing was, I had no way of getting there.

Brenda was the one who came up with the dandy solution. Her father worked as a mechanic in St. Albert. He drove back and forth every day. I could go out with him on Friday evening and come back again early Monday morning when he drove back into work. She could get it all set up, she said, no problem.

Of course, I wanted to spend the weekend at Simon's Bay really bad. But after Brenda came and said she could fix up the transportation part of it, then it was like it got to be her invitation, not Gerard's any longer.

By that time she had been in the picture for about two weeks. If you wants to know the truth about who she was—well, to put it simple—Brenda was the first girl I ever really had the hots on.

There was no big lot to the way we met. She didn't come running out of a grassy field in slow motion, ready to sling her arms around me. She was Gerard's cousin, and somehow she was there pretty often when we got together, hanging around the corridors in school. I could see it right away —not just that I liked her the first time I seen her, but that she really liked me. You can tell that in a girl a mile off.

I was never much of it until the last year or so when it came to dealing with females. It's not that easy. There's a lot more to it than I figured. You can't expect to leave them on the other side of the room anymore. Suddenly they're right up close to you and you got to look them square in the eyes.

What I seen when I looked at Brenda was pretty good, I got to say that. I won't go into any of the details, but see her in a dress like she was at the first school dance, and I tell you, you wouldn't ask no questions.

She was pretty nice all right. The only thing about it was that she was taller than me, even with the boots I had on. Damn the hormones, or whatever they're called. I mean, that's when you could really use height, when you're dancing the slow ones with a girl. I couldn't give a darn any other time. But at least you wants to come close to being even when you're there together on the dance floor. We wasn't the only ones like it, thank God. But it's still the shits, no matter how you looks at it.

I tried to forget about that part. If she didn't mind, then I sorta didn't. It never stopped me from having a good time. That's one thing about me now, there's not much problem in the asking part of getting girls to dance. I use to be like the guys you'll see who comes to a school dance and sticks in the corner all night or are all the time going outside for a smoke. They just haven't got the nerve to ask a girl, even when they're all dying to be asked. But sure once you've done it a few times, then there's shag all to it. I still ain't so hot on the slow ones myself. But I'm getting better at it. With your arms around someone like Brenda, then you tries to learn fast.

At it turned out, during the first school dance I spent practically the whole night with her. Hardly danced with any other girl. And I didn't mind that one bit. After all, she was really something, like I said.

Ay, don't get me wrong. She didn't have me twisted around her little finger. I could a been dancing with all kinds of other girls if I wanted to. Or not danced at all for that matter. It's just that sometimes you sticks with one, and that's easier. And I did get a few great kisses out of it too. Before she got aboard the bus for home. She was no slouch when it came to that, either.

That night, after I came in the house and went to bed, I got to thinking a lot about what happened. Cripes, I thought, what am I getting myself into? Did I really want to get tied onto this one girl? I felt like that was the way it could turn out to be if I let it. It was awful tough to have to decide when you never came up against a problem like that before.

After a while thinking it over, I began to fall off to sleep. I was tired, but what kept me half awake was all these wild thoughts that started running around in my head about me and Brenda. Some of them was just about as private as you can get. And my hands under the covers didn't do much to stop them. No need to say any more than that. It'd only get me embarrassed.

When I woke up the next morning all I could feel was my underwear wet and sticking to me. Make no wonder, considering the dream I had after I went to sleep. It didn't bother me much. I knew what was going on and it happened before, anyway. The worst lousy thing was the stains it made. Thank heavens for the guy who invented printed sheets.

I don't like to say it, but sometimes sex and all that goes with it can scare the shit out of a guy. I mean, I'm normal and all that, but you hardly knows what to do sometimes. I've been feeling it more and more over the past few months. I'm getting more erections than I've ever had before, especially when I wakes up in the morning. Just guaranteed, guaranteed to be hard, especially if I've been dreaming. Erection—that sounds pretty scientific. That's a word I picked up in a film we had in guidance class a couple of years ago. Us fellows started using it all the time after we had the class. Just for a laugh. I knew most of what they showed in the films anyway, but I'm glad I seen them because the way they showed it sorta tied everything together. And now I knows all the goings on with regards to females too.

But still, like I said, sometimes sex can scare the shit out of a fellow. The thing is—you've got all this information, plus you knows what you feels like yourself, and then you got to figure out how to go about dealing with it. And then again, just how much of it have girls got on their minds.

Sure, you can carry on a lot. Take a gawk at all the sexy magazines you can lay your hands on. Tell dirty jokes. Fire around comments. The fellows our age, the way we talks among ourselves, you'd think we was already all a bunch of sex maniacs.

But actually being with a girl, all that is different. If you really likes her, you don't go on with all kinds of dirt because she's liable to drop you faster than she would a stick of dynamite. It's just that it gets to the point where you're not sure what you should be saying to them or what you should be doing. These days it almost makes you wonder whether or not you're normal if sex is not on your mind all the time when you're alone with a girl.

Well, as far as me and Brenda was concerned, there wasn't chance enough for it to become much of a problem. We wasn't together long enough for that. As you probably guessed, I didn't make it out to Simon's Bay to stay for the weekend like I wanted to. And the way I got turned down loused up my life in the house even more than it was already.

I talked it over with Gerard and Brenda, and that afternoon when I went back to the house I asked Aunt Ellen if I could go. I told her who Gerard was, how everything was all set, what time I would be going and getting back, all that. She didn't say yes or no. All she would say was that I'd have to ask the army sergeant first. I might a known.

When supper was cleared away that night and I knew that he was by himself in the living room, I went in to put the question to him. He was lying back on the chesterfield reading the newspaper. There was no sense beating around the bush. I came right out with it—the same thing I said to Aunt Ellen.

He looked at me, never stopped to think about it for one second, and said, "No."

Not another word. Just no. And went back to

reading the newspaper then. Like he was a judge in the supreme court or something. Sure b'y, I thought, play the big boss. But if you thinks you're going to get away with it that easy, then you got another think coming.

"Why not?"

He looked up again. "Because I don't want you to," he said, as if those few words settled it all.

"That's no reason," I answered him back.

He put the paper down altogether and then sat up straight. He kept the same smart-aleck sound in his voice though. That didn't change. "Okay, you want a good enough reason. Well, for one thing, it's too far. For another, I don't know who this Gerard fellow you're talking about is. He might live in a tar-paper shack for all anyone knows. And for another, I don't see any need of it. That's three reasons. Good enough?"

I felt like ripping out a bloody big curse.

"They're all foolishness."

"Michael!" he raised his voice.

"Well it is! Gerard is a good friend of mine. And he don't live in no tar-paper shack like you said!"

"Now, look, I don't want to have to get mad with you." As if he wasn't already.

"But you won't even listen to me."

"Michael!" His voice was turning hard and sharp. He was trying to cover up some of his temper. "Now, I've said all I'm going to say about it. You might as well get it out of your mind. Even though you're not my son, you know, I'm still responsible for you. That's something you haven't taken time to realize. Now, I know all that's happened over the past few months hasn't been easy. But you're living with us now and you're going to have to learn to accept what I say as being the best thing for you. You might not like it, but it's the best thing.

"Now I don't want to hear you raise your voice to me again like you just did. The answer is no, you're not allowed to go. That's final. Now, go to your room and think about what I said."

I had to stand there like a fool and take that. I had a mind to tell him right off, call him right down to the dirt. He probably would a tried to clobber me if nothing else worked. I wouldn't doubt it one bit. That oversize pig! Cripes! He was bloody well right I wasn't his son. And that wasn't half of it.

I took off for the room. It was no blessed good arguing. More sense in a lousy bag of nails. I wouldn't a minded if he had said no and had some good reasons to back it up. But there wasn't one grain of sense in anything that he said. He only done it to make me spitey. I knew before I ever started just what his answer was going to be. He just wanted to show how bloody fast he could squash me into the ground with his thumb.

The best thing for me, my arse. The best thing for him was more like it. And he expected me to have some respect for him then. Not to raise my voice at him. Cripes, what made him so special?

What about him raising his voice at me? What about that? And I didn't owe him nothing, not one lousy red cent.

Curtis heard it. The bedroom door was open. He didn't say anything when I came steaming into the room. I wanted to slam the door so hard that the bloody hinges would drop off.

"What a friggin old man you got!" I had to force myself to hold everything else in. Otherwise I might a said something I would a been sorry for.

I must a been lying on the bed for an hour before I moved. I went over and over in by mind just how much I hated that godforsaken hole I had to live in. I wished to hell I could get out of it.

The first thing I done when I got up was to take a piece of paper and sit down and try to write a letter to Aunt Flo. I had it all down that I wanted to come back. That nothing was working out right. That I would promise not to be any trouble. Then I took the letter, balled it up and fired it into the garbage can. It didn't sound right. Frig, none of it was right. It was like I was begging for a chance to live with them.

Then I took another sheet of paper and started a letter to Brent. I didn't get very far with that one either, before it ended up in the garbage can. Not a darn thing was going down on the paper the way I wanted it to.

I started another one. This time it was to Grandfather that I tried to write. He was the easiest one for me to say stuff to. But it was just as well if I wrote the man in the moon. What I ended up writing him was a stupid few words asking what the weather was like, what was he doing, and all that crap. Not a word about the way I was feeling. It was a bloody waste of a stamp. But I got one and stuck it on and walked down to the drugstore and fired the letter in the mailbox.

10

The next day, Friday, I told Gerard and Brenda that I couldn't go. I wasn't allowed. That was the end of it as far as I was concerned. I could a skinned out to Simon's Bay on Saturday if I wanted to bad enough. Hitchhiked there and not one person could a stopped me. But I'd still have to come back and live with the grouch.

Brenda didn't give up that easy, though. She had it in her mind that she wanted some way of seeing me on the weekend. Of course, she didn't come right out and say so. But she throwed enough hints and looks around. I wasn't that stun. Maybe, she said, she'd be coming into St. Albert shopping with her mother on Saturday and she'd probably be staying overnight with her aunt who lived on O'Leary Street. And maybe she'd see me sometime Saturday. There's a movie we can see Saturday night, I said.

So that Saturday night me and Brenda went to the movie together. I never told anybody in the house where I was going, not even Curtis. It was

none of anybody's business except mine. The movie
we went to see was *The Apes, Part III*.

We watched it all. It was dumb enough for a
laugh, I can say that much for it. There's only so
much of this ape stuff you can take and not get
bored. We wasn't up in the back row loving it up
like you might think. I hardly knew the girl. I
knows that don't stop some fellows. But me, I
figures I should at least know the girl. We did get
around to holding hands. Big deal.

Some guys figure looks counts for everything.
I don't, although it's hard to think any other way
when you sees a nice piece of stuff in a bathing
suit stretched out on the beach. For me, personality
counts for a good bit too. And what got me latched
onto Brenda was that she had both of it. In the
looks department she was right up there. Down a
few notches from Sandra Colbourne maybe, but
still pretty nice. And she had to have a great
personality if the way she acted with me was
anything to go by.

We spent half the time after the movie talking
about skidoos, for God's sake. Most girls, all they
wants to talk about is school or T.V. programs or
things like that, but there was me and Brenda
gabbing on and on about skidoos and ice fishing.
Maybe she was only doing it to play up to me. I
dunno. I couldn't care less, anyway. Cripes, you
knows it wouldn't a been the fun having her
along, the way we use to swish around on the
skidoos in back of Marten last winter.

Brenda was a real nice girl all right. It's not every day you runs across girls like her. Sometimes when I starts talking to someone I likes, I can't get stopped. That was the way it was with Brenda. I went to work and told her everything. I really did. I went on and on like I'd never shut up. I told her about the accident and she almost bawled right there on the spot. She was the first person I ever felt like I could tell it to.

And I never stopped there. I yacked on about moving to St. Albert and how I hated being at Curtis' place because of his old man. I told her then just how it happened that he wouldn't let me go out to Simon's Bay that weekend. If anyone had yacked on and on to me that much I would a told them to shut up. But all she done was listen and hold my hand real tight in hers.

Well, we must a been there in the trees out back of the ball field for I guess almost two hours. The most we done was talk. We got around to hugging up to each other because it was a bit chilly, and we went pretty long on the mouth to mouth sessions a few times, but really the most we done was talk.

When she finally did look at her watch and found out that it was after midnight, she just about had a copper kitten. She made me get up right away and start walking back home with her. Her aunt would be fierce if she came home too late. Maybe she'd never get to stay there another weekend.

All the way up the sidewalk along Alexander Street we was laughing like crazy, running sometimes, she dragging me by the hand, me wasting time by trying to tell her I had twisted my ankle. Cripes, if anyone heard us they must a thought we was cracked. Too bad.

We turned into O'Leary Street and got to about two houses away from her aunt's place. We could see the lights on—her aunt probably still waiting up for her. She told me to go back the other way, not for me to pass in front of the house. That would make it all the harder to explain why she was so late.

"Hey, wait a minute," I called out to her as she took off walking fast towards the house and left me standing alone in the middle of the sidewalk.

"What is it?" She turned her head back to answer me, still moving.

"Wait. Wait."

"Hurry up, what is it? I'll be killed."

"This," I said, running up to her. I stopped, took her head real nice in my two hands and laid a long and easy one on her lips.

Then I turned around and walked away. Slow, like it was something I could a been doing every day of the week.

"Hey," she said. It was the only thing she could think of. I guess the old romantic cat had been too much for her.

"Yeah," I looked around, smiling.

"See ya," she said.

"Take it easy," I said, and put up my hand to her. She waved back to me.

She went on walking then up to her aunt's place. I took off and ran back down the street like my arse was on fire. For no other reason than I felt like running. Never stopped, either, till I'd run all the way down two streets. And yelling. Because I felt like that too. I let out the bloody big yell as if I'd just won a hundred thousand dollars in the lottery.

St. Albert, you stinks! You stinks! Up yours with ten million telephone poles. Old man, you stinks the worst of the lot. Suffer, old man, suffer.

I was making him suffer all right. It was twelve-thirty then. Already they'd been doing a lot of wondering about where I was. They didn't have a clue, not a clue. And that was the way it was going to stay until I was ready to go home.

I must a walked five miles or more. To places I'd never even been to in car. I must a looked in every god-blessed store window in the place. I seen every cop car, that was for sure. Some of them giving me only just enough time to skin out and around a building.

When I marched into the house finally, it was after two o'clock, the latest I ever stayed out. Aunt Ellen was just about off her head. She had herself worried sick. I really was sorry she had to go through all that. The old man was still out driving around, looking for me. The cops had been called in on it too.

I told her I lost my way. That was a stupid lie. She knew it. So I told her I was out for a walk, which was true, in a way. I said to her that I was sorry, that I didn't mean for her to have to get so upset like that.

I never said any more. I went into the bedroom and closed the door. When the old man came roaring home, saying that he still hadn't seen me, I was already in bed. He came storming into the room just as soon as Aunt Ellen had it out about what happened.

He banged open the door and switched on the light.

"You weren't out for no walk at three o'clock in the goddamn morning, now where were you!" He was savage with me all right, no two ways about it.

I sat up in bed. "I was so out for a walk. Anyway, it's not three o'clock yet. It's only two-thirty."

"You little bugger! Don't you dare answer me back like that. Where were you? I've got half the lousy cops in this place out looking for you. Aunt Ellen was just about gone crazy wondering where you were."

"I told her I was sorry."

"Sorry! Lord God, what the hell is the sense of you! Are you gone nuts or what! If Curtis had done anything like that I goddamn well wouldn't be wasting my breath. I'd have his ass red enough by now. And I got a damn good mind to try it on you."

"Don't dare . . ."

"You little bugger. Jeeesus!" While he was dragging out that last word he held up his fist and left it shaking in the air. Aunt Ellen was there holding him back. It really looked like he was itching to hit me.

I threw back the covers and hopped outa bed. All I had on was a pair of shorts. I didn't give a shit about that.

"Com'on, com'on, hit me!" My fists was wrung up tight as hammers hanging down by my sides. "Com'on, com'on, see how fast you can pound me out. Someone who's not even half your size."

If you ever seen anyone bursting with spite, it was him. He was blood red. One smack from that fist of his was all it would a took to flatten me out. I knew that. I wasn't worried. He couldn't be that much of a lunatic to get himself hauled into court. I'd have him there pretty fast if he ever tried it. What he had in his mind when he came through the door was to scare me. Well, I didn't scare that easy. He wasn't dealing with Curtis this time. And he knew it too.

Aunt Ellen tried to get in between us. "We'll talk about it in the morning," she said. "That's enough fuss for one night, Ted. Ted, please! You better go out and call the police and tell them that it's okay."

He was looking to find some way for him to back down and not let everyone think he was giving in to her. He ripped off another curse and bolted out the room just as quick as he came in.

I was left standing there in front of Aunt Ellen, and Curtis lying in bed, and now Marie in the doorway. They was all staring at me there with hardly any clothes on.

"Go back to bed, Michael," she said. She went over to the door, pushed Marie out, and closed it. I flicked off the light and crawled in under the covers again.

I hadn't been out for revenge. I was out to show him that he just couldn't go pushing me around for no reason.

I didn't know what Curtis thought of it all. We never said anything to each other even though we was both lying there in bed awake. I wasn't in any mood to talk about it. I was just hoping that it stuck in his mind what his old man had said about if it had been him and not me.

11

All the next week I was thinking about home, my real home. Especially after I got the letter from Grandfather. That made me want to go back so bad I could feel it eating away at my guts. Grandfather mentioned about how the squid was in and how him and Brent was going out to jig some. He never tried to make it sound like a big deal. And I knew for why, too—because he figured the more he said about it, the more I would be longing to come back. But just the mention of it was enough for me. I knows if it had been up to Grandfather I would never a left Marten in the first place.

Since I'd come to St. Albert, I'd gotten two letters from him. And there was a part on the end of each one that Brent had put there—big-size letters, with a few sentences filling up half a page. The letter I sent back to them this time was the longest one I ever wrote.

I never was so hot when it came to writing letters. The most I ever done was in school, like when you had to write to some fake cousin way the dyins over in Saskatchewan somewhere, thanking him for this Christmas present and asking him why didn't he come over and pay you a visit during the summer holidays. That kinda stuff. Or a few times I wrote for something out of a magazine.

This letter was long, but once I got it going there was no trouble getting the words down. I wrote it like it came straight out of my mouth. The only thing was, I had to be careful what I said because I knew that more than likely Aunt Flo would be reading it too. After I finished, I took it and read it over and I seen that it came out pretty strong about how bad I missed the place. I must a asked a million questions about what everybody was doing. I had questions down about practically every person I ever use to hang around with. And I'd told Brent that *he* was the one who had to learn to stick it out. Some bluff I was.

"Stick it out" was the words for it all right. After the little incident in the bedroom, the old man and me hardly spent two seconds in the same room together, except for mealtimes. And even when we was forced to sit down to the same table to eat, we hardly so much as looked at each other. That was some way to have to live with anybody, now wasn't it.

I had to have something to take my mind off it. Brenda was what done that for me. After the Saturday night of the long talk, Brenda and me was right into it, thick and heavy. I had my mind made up that it was okay for me to be hanging around with just one girl all the time. Actually, I never thought I'd see the day when I'd be so caught up with only one female. Getting together between classes, notes to each other, the whole bit. Cripes, it started to look like I'd been at it all my life, the way I was playing the real love nut.

I figured I had to be careful, though. You gotta watch yourself in these things. After a while, if you're not on your guard, it could get so that they thinks they owns you. I seen that happen to a friend of mine once. He's sixteen. He broke up with this one named Linda and she had the biggest kinda bawl over it. She kept phoning him up all the time even though he told her to get lost. See, girls can take things too serious. I bet you a darn that some of them even after the first date starts thinking about what it would be like to be married to you and all kinds of crap like that.

I figured that if Brenda ever did get too wound up over me, then I'd just maybe have to cut it off for a while. Get myself a little room to breathe. I'd be careful, though, to see that she wouldn't take it too hard.

All this was some of what was going on in my head. The problem was, I liked the girl. I really did like the girl. For frig's sake, I thought, maybe I'm in love with her. And when you're in love with someone you don't give too much of a darn about whether or not she's too wound up with you. Now do you? Shit, see how mixed up I was.

One thing I did know for sure—I wasn't too fussy about some of the things girls'll do if they likes you. Some girls have this stupid way of showing other people they're hooked up with somebody. They'll mark their school books all up. That's a sure sign of something—every square inch of white space inside their books filled in. So-and-so loves so-and-so. Inside hearts, around in circles, up one side of the page, down the other. No such thing as being secret about it. I believe they must change books when they changes boyfriends. I don't get off on that atall. It's like they've captured you and got their branding iron put to work.

In St. Albert, another thing was the song dedications on the radio. The big event to look forward to on Friday nights was eleven o'clock to one when the radio station would play requests and announce who phoned in to have them dedicated and to who. Sometimes I'd listen to part of it in bed with the transistor radio I had. I'd rig it up with the earphone. I wore out more batteries that way—falling asleep with the radio still on.

The Friday after me and Brenda went to the movie I was lying there half-asleep when I just about had a heart attack right there in the bed. "Going out especially to Michael from Brenda Lambert," the fellow said, "I Only Want To Be With You." I just about keeled right over, that's the god's truth.

Cripes, that kinda thing can really shake a fellow up when he's not expecting it. I couldn't get a wink of sleep for the next two hours. It wasn't the idea of it so much that got to me. I mean, it was pretty nice of her and all to be thinking about it. And words like that said a lot about how much she thought of me. Too bloody much, maybe. What really got me was the fact that she had to broadcast it all over the globe. Every girl in school and half the fellows had their ears bolted onto that program. Sure she might just as well have rented a loudspeaker and paraded all day long around the school blasting it out.

Maybe she didn't mean it like that. Maybe she picked out that song because she liked the music. Perhaps the words wasn't the main thing atall. But it was the words that was ringing through my head the whole blessed night. It could be I was making a big deal out of it for nothing. It could just a been one bit of that craziness girls figures they got to do. Whether it was or not, I sure had a label now. Just the same as having B-R-E-N-D-A stamped in fifty-foot letters across my forehead.

On Monday morning, when I went inside the school door, the first thing I caught sight of was a crowd of girls all bunched into one corner having their gossip hour. The one that stuck out was Juanita Hickey, mainly because she had the biggest mouth. If there was ever a girl that was a pure pain, it was Juanita Hickey. Her name alone was enough to give you the creeps. Sounded like something you'd want to build a barbwire fence around. Juanita, the big tongue, comes right up to me the first thing and says, "How's Brenda, Michael," and laughs and giggles in a way that made me want to sock her a good one right between the eyes.

Not a damn word could I get out. Cripes, I should at least a been able to get out something. But no sir, not a word. If I had my time back I would a told her to go stuff her face with rotten eggs or some other brilliant thing like that. But no, all I done was walk by like an idiot and turn red. Red, for frig's sake, me turning red on account of Juanita Hickey. Cripes, her! Sure she had a face on her like a turbot. She was that much of a pain that if you fired her into a barrel of pickle she'd make it boil over.

It didn't stop there, either. The whole morning I was getting all kinds of these stupid comments. Some of them only said it once, for a joke. I didn't mind that. I'm not someone who can't take a joke. But if there's one thing I can't stand, it's for someone to be teasing and then be keeping it up and keeping it up. That drives me, that does.

Brenda, Brenda, Brenda. All the time it was one person or another. I couldn't even concentrate on the work I was sposed to be doing. After recess it got worse. The whole lousy two periods we had before dinner I could hear her name trailing up from the back of the classroom. I had a darn good idea who it was even before I caught him at it.

The first few times I looked back he managed to cover it up and I couldn't say for sure who it might be. But the fourth time when I turned my head around, I caught him with his big mouth open—Kentson. It looked like he hadn't learned much from the first lesson I tried to teach him.

That was the only trouble I had since the time I belted him the second day of school. He'd stayed away from me like I had the plague. Then that morning there he was with the face going again. I spose he figured that since everyone else was having something to say, then he could join it too and I wouldn't notice it. Not too friggin likely.

Now let me get this straight once and for all. I don't get into fights because I wants to be at it. I don't go beating up on people for no reason. Maybe I do have a bit of a temper sometimes, but I was hardly ever into a fight when I lived home, except for a few scraps when I was younger, and everyone gets into them. I don't get no thrills out of it. But there sure as hell comes a time when a fellow can only take so much.

Kentson was getting to me with that foolishness. He was the only one at it anymore. A couple of times between periods I told him to cut it out. Then the other fellows started getting on my back because it was like I really must a had something going with Brenda. And that made Kentson do it all the more.

Maybe I wouldn't a minded if it had been anybody but him. As soon as the bell rang for dinner and the teacher went through the door, I gave him fair warning.

"Kentson," I said, getting up from my seat, "you keep your tongue quiet if you knows what's good for you."

Him and his two stupid friends was still in the back of the classroom. Right away they started to laugh.

"I *knows* what's good for me," he said.

I couldn't be positive that he was making fun or not.

"Yeah," I said, "well, you just better do it."

He had to see that I was getting mad. I would a been satisfied to let what he said go by. And I'm sure that he wouldn't a said anything else, except that his jerky friends was there with him.

"Or what?" said one of them.

I started to walk down between the seats. "Or I'll pound him like I done before."

Kentson had one of two choices. Either he'd let it pass and look chicken in front of the others. Or he'd say something back.

"Yeah!" he said, like he was something tough.

"Yeah!" I said, even louder.

"Take more than a stupid baywop like you to do it."

The other jerks snickered.

I stood there and glared at him. When I didn't say anything to him right away, then he got it into his head that he just might be able to get away with a little more.

"You and that dumb broad of yours are a good pair all right."

Lord holy dyin! You thinks I didn't lay my fist into him nar bit fast! One smack was all it took. I sent him sailing back over the seats with one ram of my fist. Cripes, you think I was going to put up with that? The stupid fool was asking for it. My fist took him in the mouth. I could feel my knuckles smash into the side of his face. His head jerked back, he stumbled on his feet and went flying backwards over the seats.

But the bloody thing was, Kentson never got up. He never moved once after his head hit the floor.

Lord dyin, you think I meant for that to happen! I never thought I hit him that hard. I really didn't. I was only out to teach him a lesson. I was really mad all right when I done it. I lost my temper. But I had a right to. How was I to know he was going to bang his stupid head on the floor.

I damn near killed him is what I done.

I stood up there like a fool. Kentson out cold on the floor. His two friends trying to see what the hell was wrong with him. And then they started shouting and yelling when he wouldn't come to. Someone took off running out the door to get the school nurse.

Then the two of them pitched right into me, saying it was all my fault.

"What in the hell did you hit him for?"

"You heard what he said."

"He was only jokin."

"It wasn't any joke."

"Who in the frig do you think you are? Don't think the cops won't get you for this."

"He's not really hurt. He only knocked hesself out when he hit the floor."

"A lot you know! He might be dead for all you care!"

"It was an accident."

"It wasn't any accident! You wanted to see him hurt, didn't you? Didn't you?"

"No, it was just a stupid accident."

"Accident! You wouldn't know an accident if you saw one. You're too friggin dumb!"

I couldn't take any more. I don't care. Call me chicken. Call me whatever the hell you wants, I don't care. I just couldn't take any more.

I ran outa the room, and so fast as I could down the corridors. I almost knocked into the school nurse when she came running out of her office. I ran right down to the exit doors, and banged them open. I took off down over the steps and out into the street.

I had to get away from them. I ran and ran until my guts was aching and my breath came in and out so hard that I had to stop. Where I got to was a park or something. I hardly knew what it was. I searched and searched and the only place I could find where there wasn't any people was down in one corner. In back of the tennis courts.

I sat down there between two maple trees and a damn big wall.

I almost bawled.

Almost, I said, almost.

12

What was pounding at me the whole time was that maybe Kentson really was dead. If he was dead, then I'd crack up. I really would. I could feel it.

But he couldn't be dead. He was just knocked out. He had to be.

And then it came back to me again. About the other accident and everything. After four months I thought it couldn't come back at me that bad anymore. But all that was inside me was tortured sick with it again. Making me want to curl up in a hole somewhere and be forgot about.

I was just a stupid fool to be fighting against it. I should be giving up and just do as I'm told. Quit trying to be the know-it-all. Learn to be one of them.

Good thing I got so cold. Good thing I ran off with no coat on and after a while I was shivering and freezing to death. Other than the cold, I don't know what could a brought me back to my right mind.

* * *

Kentson wasn't dead. But he was in the hospital with a concussion. I talked to someone on the way back who told me that. I knew he couldn't be dead. It would a had to be some bang on the head for him to be dead.

It was bad enough that he was in the hospital. And it was all because of me that he was there. A little fight means nothing. But to send someone to the hospital, that's something else. And I knew they'd be saying it like, "He must be crazy. Sure he hit him that hard that they had to take him to the hospital. He almost killed him, I wouldn't doubt." That's what they'd be saying about me.

I made up my mind to go right back to the school. I knew there'd have to come a time when I would face the principal anyway, so it was just as well to get it over with.

I made my way down through the corridors towards his office. I tried not to look at anyone. The corridors was packed with students waiting to go into class. I picked a lousy time, just before the bell was to go for the first period in the afternoon. I kept looking straight ahead. I didn't so much as say hello to Gerard when he called out to me.

"Sellers is looking for you," he said. I didn't need anyone to tell me that.

I turned in and around the corner to his office. I stopped by the sign telling me it was the reception desk. A secretary was typing inside. She didn't notice me there. I could see that the door to his office was part way open, so I walked around the desk and on in towards it.

I walked right into the middle of a conversation Sellers was having with a cop. Both of them turned their heads and stared at me.

"I guess you wants to see me, Mr. Sellers," I said quietly.

"I do?"

He didn't even know who I was.

"I'm the fellow who was in the fight with Lewis Kentson."

"You are?"

"Yes, sir."

"Officer, this is the boy we've been discussing."

Cripes, he got the cops in on it too. First when I seen the cop it never came to me that I was the reason he was there.

I never had any dealings with Sellers before. I seen him around enough to know who he was. That was about it. You don't get to know the principal in a big school like that. Not like in the school home. Unless you gets sent to his office. Then you gets to know him quick enough. I didn't think he could a been real hard on students though, because I never heard any of the boys say that he was.

Lots of fellows would a been scared outa their minds if they was put in the situation I was in. Having to face a cop and the principal like that after what happened. I'll admit that I was far from calm about it all. But I did have enough sense in me to keep a clear head. I was going to get what I had to say to come out right.

As long as Sellers was fair about it. Some principals would jump down your throat right away without even listening to your side of the story. Some would figure they should get raving mad just to scare the hell outa you so you'd never do it again. I was willing to be honest about the whole thing. I'd tell them the way it happened if they'd just listen.

I didn't know if he was putting on a big act for the cop or if that was the way he went about things all the time, but first what he done was ask me to please sit down. He didn't tell me, he asked me in a quiet voice to please sit down. Then he got up and closed his office door.

He sat down again behind his desk in his swivel chair. The cop was across from the desk on one side and I was on the other.

He looked at me. "Now, Michael, before I say anything to you, I want you to tell us in your own words exactly what happened. Nobody'll interrupt you until you're finished."

He leaned back in the chair away from the desk and folded his arms. He stared at me, then nodded for me to start.

God, I thought, this is better than I expected. I'll have all the chance in the world to say what I wants. I was a little bit shaky first. Starting off and all, especially where it was the bit about Brenda and why they was teasing me. I tried to make it sound important, how teasing can get under your skin. People when they gets older don't realize that. They don't have it done to them anymore. And then I told them how the fight started. I didn't try to lie. I told them I punched Kentson for what he said. I didn't know he was going to hurt himself, I really didn't.

They listened. They didn't say a word the whole time, like he promised. All Sellers done was stare at me with his arms folded across his chest. His expression never changed once. A couple of times the cop wrote something down in his notebook.

When I finished, Sellers asked me if I had any more to say.

"No, sir." I was polite all the way through. I wasn't one bit saucy to him.

"You realize, of course, that Lewis is in the hospital," Sellers said, his arms still folded.

"Yes, sir, I believe he has a small concussion, sir."

"Not very small, Michael. He'll be in the hospital for a week or more."

He waited. "Do you have anything more to add about that?"

"No sir . . . I mean, I didn't think he was going to hurt himself like he done, sir. It was an accident."

"If it was such an accident, Michael, what was the reason you ran away?"

I wasn't expecting that. And he said it so fast that it threw my thinking right off.

"I was scared."

"Scared? Why should you be scared if it was an accident? You said it was an accident, didn't you?"

Shit, now he's started, I thought to myself. Yes, you knows I said it was a friggin accident. I said that to myself too. I started to swear in my own mind.

"I was scared his buddies might turn on me, sir." Now I was beginning to lie.

"A brave fellow like you? Someone who didn't mind starting a fight with the three fellows all there?"

He was making a move to pick me apart. I might a known the way he was first off was too good to be true. He was coming on with this big smart-alecky voice. That got on my bloody nerves.

I stopped answering his questions cause they was getting me all confused. Then I realized that it only made matters worse. Like by that he had proved his point.

"Young man . . ." he started again.

Oh, frig no, here it comes now for sure. He was getting into the "young man" shit with me.

". . . this is the second time you've been caught fighting inside the school building. Mr. Bartlett, your English teacher, tells me he saw you fighting with Lewis once before, only the second day after school opened this year."

"But that . . ." I interrupted.

"Let me finish, please. He says that he saw you fighting. Another teacher supported him in what he said. Now, I must be truthful, other than that incident we have not had any problems with you this year. In fact, several of the teachers have commented to me that you show good interest in your school work.

"But—and this is a very big but—what has happened today is a very serious matter. We are not talking about a little argument in the corridor. We are not even talking about one boy giving another boy a few bruises. What we are talking about is someone being hurt so bad that he has to be admitted to the hospital with a concussion. I hope you realize how serious this is. This could have put you in a court of law. Fortunately for you, the boy's parents do not want to press charges. But that still does not excuse you from what happened."

"Sir . . ." I tried to break in. He was making me out to be some kind of criminal. I didn't try to hurt Kentson, I told him that enough times.

"Please let me finish. You had your chance to say what you wanted. Isn't that right?"

I didn't answer him.

"Now, as far as the school is concerned, we must take steps to see that this type of incident does not happen again. We cannot have these things going on inside the school building.

"You say it was an accident. It may be possible

that it was, but that remains to be proven. Two facts, however, are very clear to me, as they must to you—you *were* fighting on school property and someone *was* seriously hurt because of your actions. I have no choice but to take measures to see that such a thing is not repeated.

"Stand up, please."

He waited till I did.

"Starting this afternoon, you are expelled from this school for a period of two weeks. You are not to return to classes until after that time. If there is any further trouble with you when you do return, then I may have to recommend to your parents that you be removed permanently from this school. You may leave now. You are excused."

Like someone hit in the head and knocked senseless, I turned and went out slowly through the office door. It was so much of a shock that I didn't know what else I could be doing.

I was out in the corridor and halfway to my locker before it came to me that I should never a been out there, that I should still be inside his office, telling him that he was all wrong. There was no reason to be kicking me outa school. I didn't do anything.

I turned around and started to go back. I went straight to the office door again and opened it. I broke in on them talking like I done before.

Sellers looked at me, waited to hear me say something. He had his bloody arms folded again. I stood there. I could hardly get it out. Cripes, there I was again, trying to push words out of my mouth.

"Sir," I said when I finally got started, "you needs to read your stupid records. You couldn't recommend a lousy thing to my parents. Both of them are dead."

I turned around then and walked through the door again, hauling it closed when I did. All I kept thinking once I got outside was why the hell did I say "sir." It shouldn't a been "sir" atall.

I moved like a friggin zombie past the few people that was in the corridor. I got to my locker, opened it, and pulled out every last thing that was in there. I don't know why I cleared it all out. The same as if it was the end of the year or something. I slammed it shut, empty. And in a few minutes I was back on the street again. This time walking with a stupid armload of books.

When it finally settled into my head what had happened, all I kept thinking was holy dyin, holy dyin, like I'd never get over the shock.

I wasn't feeling mad anymore. I was too stunned to be mad. Being kicked outa school mightn't sound like much to some people. Some fellows would a laughed in his face and been happy as hell to get some holidays. But nothing like that had ever happened to me before. In Marten I got along with the principal the best kind. Never once was I ever in any trouble like that at school.

I wasn't mad. I wasn't scared. I don't know what

the frig I was. All mixed up again, I guess, all mixed up in the head. I walked around with all those stupid books in my arms for two hours. Two hours. Because I didn't want to go to the house and explain it to Aunt Ellen. I wasn't scared to. I just didn't much like the idea of trying to explain something like that with just us in the house at two o'clock in the afternoon. She'd probably be making something in the kitchen. I didn't want to have to go in the house and try to explain it all to her while she was in the kitchen baking and her hands all full of flour or something. Cripes, wasn't that dumb. How stupid. But I didn't want to have to explain things while she was there all busy at something else.

I went to the hospital. I walked all the way across to the other side of the city to the hospital. Almost didn't go in the door. Because if there's anything I can't stand, it's hospitals. When I did go in, I went straight to the information desk and piled up this stupid stack of school books. The girl looked at me like I was nuts. I told her I wanted to find out how Kentson was. Only I said Lewis Kentson.

That would be on the fourth floor and would I like to go up? No, I only wanted to find out how he was. I have all these stupid books to carry around, you see.

She rang up to the fourth floor. The nurse told her that he had improved a lot in the last hour. That's what she said to me. And I said that's all I wanted to know. And thank you. I have to go on with all these books now. Thank you.

She looked at me and laughed. She didn't look at me with some weird expression and shake her head like you might expect. She looked at me and laughed.

I walked all the way back across the city to the beginning of the street where the house was. It was still too early to go in. I made a detour down another street and out around until I came to Kelly's drugstore. What I done was plank all the books on top of the mailbox and stayed there leaning against it. My arms ached. I never went inside the drugstore at all. I leaned up against the mailbox for a while, and then I took my history book from the top of the pile and sat down on the sidewalk with it. I sat there by the lousy mailbox with the history book and started to look through it. Do you believe that? I wasn't mad or nervous or scared. I was just sitting there by the mailbox with my stupid history book open in front of me.

13

I had a good idea before I even went into the house what was in store for me there. There mightn't be much before the old man came home. But then watch out.

Aunt Ellen knew about what happened already. Sellers had phoned the house from school and she'd gotten another call from Mrs. Kentson. I told her I wanted to wait till he came home. I'd only have to repeat it all over again. She said no, she wanted to hear it now. So I told her. Curtis was there in the kitchen too, trying to say what he could to back me up. I shouldn't a needed any help from him. I told her the truth plain and simple. And if the truth didn't show that what happened to Kentson was an accident, then it was just too bad. She couldn't be blind as a bat like Sellers.

When I finished, what she said was, "That's your side of the story, is it, Michael?"

"No, it's not my side of the story! It's what happened!" I lost my temper. I didn't mean to.

I shouted at her. It was just that I got so bloody mad at the way she said it. Like I'd have to pass a dozen lousy lie-detector tests before she'd believe either word I said.

"Mrs. Kentson's version of the story is a bit different. She said to me on the phone that you've been bothering Lewis since the first day of school."

Bothering Lewis! What the hell was that supposed to mean? Me bothering him! What about the other way around? Now I knew what I done was the right thing. I should a smashed his lying face in a bit more.

"That's a lie," I told her. "Idn't it Curtis? Curtis knows. Curtis knows what he's like."

"Mom, you can't believe that. Kentson is a liar. *He's* the one who is always causing trouble."

"All I know is what Mrs. Kentson told me. And I was talking to Mrs. Morris and Mrs. Simmons as well."

"You sure picked the right ones!" I was yelling again. I couldn't control myself. "And what did Sellers tell you? I spose he said it was all my fault. I spose you're ready to believe every lousy word they says. What do you think I'm telling you if it's not the truth? Why should I have to lie!"

"Michael, stop yelling. Please! I didn't say you were lying."

"Well, you said the next thing to it."

"Michael, all I'm saying is, according to everybody else I've been talking to, this would not have happened if it wasn't for you. They said

Lewis would not have been hurt at all except for you starting it."

"Me starting it! He was the one who had his lousy big mouth goin!" I shouted at her. I got so bloody mad. Some people wouldn't believe you, not if they seen you swear on the Bible.

"Michael, that's not much of a reason to put someone in the hospital."

Shit! It was just as well to be talking to the side of the wall. Just as well. The hell with it. I wasn't about to waste my breath any longer. I stamped off outa the kitchen, went into the bedroom and slammed the door.

Not one lousy person believed what I said except Curtis. And that was only because he was in the school and he knew the rights of everything. That's what bugs me! Every friggin time the ones that thinks they knows it all are the ones who are never there when it happens. And Sellers, he didn't have two clues anyway about what went on outside his office. Just because they're older, they thinks they're the ones who knows better.

And the bloody worst was yet to come. Wait till it got around to the time for the old man to have his say. That was going to be something. I could see it coming now.

After a while Curtis came in and sat down on the other bed across from me. He was the only sensible one I'd seen all day. He told me he had a long talk with his mother about what Kentson was really like. I doubt if it done much good.

"Curtis," I said, "what would you do if you was me?" Me asking him for advice. Now that was something.

"Keep telling them the way it really happened. That's all you can do. Eventually they'll have to see that you're right."

"The friggin truth don't work around here. They wants to see me lyin right through my teeth."

"Mike, be careful with the old man. Don't say too much to him for your own good. He's going to be breathin fire when he hears about this."

"Screw the old man."

Right away I apologized. I shouldn't a said it. It was just that I was in such a rotten mood. I thought, shit, I would a nailed anyone who said anything like that to me about my father. I would a flattened him right on.

Curtis never got mad. He just looked at me. "Forget it, Mike."

The big showdown started at six.

No sense trying to describe how he reacted to the news about me when Aunt Ellen spilled it out to him. If you had an atomic bomb and exploded it next to the kitchen sink you might a had something to compare it to.

After about five minutes of the smoke and fire, me and Curtis went out into the hallway. We stopped before we came to the kitchen.

"What's that kid trying to prove now! What's he got for sense!" I heard him say. "Kentson—he sure picked a fine one. Father a superintendent at the plant. Uncle the mayor. That's sure going to do one hell of a lot for my business. Both of them have bought new cars from me every year for the past ten years. Business is bad enough as it is. Jesus, that young bugger is going to apologize to them if it's the last thing he does. Where is he?"

"Now, Ted, get a hold of yourself," Aunt Ellen said. Useless words, if there ever was any.

Curtis grabbed my arm, trying not to let me go in there, but I pushed him away and burst in on them in the kitchen.

"I'm right here. And before anyone goes one step farther, I'm going to have my say about the whole thing."

It startled him the way I came in so fast. He was still dressed in the overcoat and suit he wore to work. I knew I had to come on strong right off the bat. Otherwise I'd never get a chance to say anything. I started off talking so quick that he had no choice but to listen to me.

"What happened today at school between me and Kentson was Kentson's fault. It would never a happened if he hadn't started it. I hit him first, but that was only because I had to. He would a kept it up all day if I hadn't shut him up. And he hurt himself only because he was stun enough to fall over a stupid desk and bang his head. If he tells you any different, or his mother, or Sellers, I don't care who it is, then they're lyin, and either

you believes them or you believes me and Curtis.
Curtis says the same thing."

He came back at me like a sledgehammer.

"I don't give a good goddamn whose fault it is!
You shouldn't have been at it in the first place.
Can you get that through your thick skull? Don't
you know any other way to settle an argument
than by bashing someone's head in?"

"Hell, the stupid jerk was mockin me, calling
me all kinds of names. What was I sposed to do,
shake hands with en?"

"Whata you mean—calling you names? Was that
all it was? Was that what it was! Jesus, you're not
a youngster anymore!"

"How would *you* like it if someone called *you* a
stupid baywop? How'd you like that? I spose you'd
let en get away with it, would ya?"

"Well, he must have had some reason for saying
it."

Cripes! I could hardly believe my friggin ears.
Some reason for it! What the dyins was he trying
to do, pick up for him!

"Whata ya mean, he must a had some reason
for it? His bloody reason was to get me mad.
That's what his bloody reason was. His stupid
arsed-up way of getting back at me."

"Michael, you cool off. You hear me? You cool
off and listen to me! And if you're not careful I'll
smack you down in that chair and make you listen.
You should be smart enough by now to know that

you had to expect some of that when you came to live in St. Albert. In a place the size of Marten people don't all speak the same as they do here. You know that. They talk different, they act different, and they don't know as much. You got to expect some people to laugh at you. It's only natural. But any sensible person would get over it. They'd change after a while. Just like you got to change and cut out your stubbornness."

"Cripes," I yelled, "you're worse than they are!"

He drew back. His stupid little pep talk was turning my guts. It made him all the madder when he seen that he couldn't pump any of that bullshit into me.

"What the hell difference do it make," I yelled, "where I comes from or what words I uses? I spose you figures that St. Albert is the only place people got any sense. Well, I'll let you in on a little secret. People here haven't got two clues compared to most people home, not two friggin clues."

I had him ripping mad, fierce altogether. He wasn't giving any heed atall to what I was saying. Not a bit, I could see it in his eyes. All that was getting through to him was the way I was saying it. Shouting. Yelling at him like it was someone my own age I was talking to. I didn't give a darn who he was or how old he was. I wasn't going to put up with him saying stuff like that. No, by cripes, I wasn't.

He reached out and grabbed me by the arm.

"Listen you! Don't you go screaming at me like

you own this goddamn house. I took you in here. And it wasn't because I had to either."

"Now Ted . . ." Aunt Ellen said.

"You shut up." He pointed his finger at her. "I've had to listen to too much from this punk already."

He turned back to me. "I took you in, not because I had to, but because you had no other place to live. You've been living here in my house and eating my food for two months. And what do you turn around and do? Kick up a fuss and start acting like you own the place. Now you listen, and you listen good. I came here to live from a place not half the size of where you came from. I came here and sweated my ass off to build up a business. I started off with seven lousy dollars twenty years ago and I built it up till I had one of the best goddamn businesses in St. Albert and one of the best homes to go with it. And if you think you can come here and do like you please, then kid you're going to have to learn to change your tune pretty fast. Nobody runs things in this house except me. You got that? Nobody! I thought a lot about your father and mother. Only for that I'd kick you out on your ass tomorrow."

All the time I was trying to haul away from the hold he had on my arm. I couldn't get away. Not until he stopped talking and then let go.

"You didn't care anything about my father and mother," I told him.

"Now, Michael, that's not true," Aunt Ellen said.

"And what's more, they didn't care anything about you. And if you don't like me here I can bloody well get out."

He tried to latch his paws around my arm again. I moved away before he had chance.

"By God, you're not going to leave then! And that's what you're not! You're going to stay here and you're going to learn to like it, you got that! You're going to learn a few goddamn manners too, and you're going to get that stubbornness outa you, even if I have to beat it out. If your old man hadn't always given you so much of your own way, you wouldn't be in the mess you're in now."

I would a come back at him for that, but he didn't give me the chance. He took one step more and shouted down at me, all the time pointing that friggin finger of his.

"And what's more, you're going to go over to Mr. Kentson's tht first thing tomorrow morning and apologize for what you did."

"Like hell I am!"

That done it. That broke everything loose. He made one lunge for me. Grabbed me by the shoulders and rammed me up against the kitchen wall! It banged the back of my head in.

"Ted!"

"You stay outa this, Ellen!"

He looked down at me. All the time I was twisting and turning to get myself free. But it didn't do no good.

His voice turned off low. He spoke at me almost

under his breath. Only loud enough for the two of us to hear. It came out through his teeth. "Michael, my boy. If you ever say that to me again, if you ever so much as think about it, so help me I'll turn you over and pound your bare ass until the blood runs out."

I was pinned solid up against the wall, my feet barely touching the floor. I had to listen to it. I had no choice. The only thing I could a done was kick him in the shins or give him the knee between the legs. But I wouldn't be the one to fight that dirty. I wouldn't give him the satisfaction of knowing I even thought of that.

He let me drop. I was so stunned where he struck my head and spitey all the one time that I hardly knew where I was going. I was halfway down the hall when I turned back and screamed, "Don't you offer to lay another finger on me! Don't you offer or I'll have the cops on you so fast it'll make your friggin head spin!"

I ran the rest of the way to the room. Slammed the door shut and locked it.

I could hear him shout, "I'm not through with you yet, kid! Not by a long shot."

That friggin blood-of-a-bitch! That bastard!

14

I was that spitey I crumpled up on the bed, drove and pounded my fist into the mattress. How much of that maniac did I have to put up with? Thought a lot of my father and mother. Like hell. Cripes, if only I could a got a good crack at him! I'd a showed him. By God, I'd a showed him.

Eat his friggin food. I wouldn't eat another lick of his friggin food, not if I was starved to death. I wasn't going to be in that house much longer. Mark my words.

I never moved from the bed. I just lay there. I must a used every curse word I knew a hundred times over. I shouldn't a been doing that. It proved he was getting to me. I thought about it— I must a cursed more in the last few weeks than I ever done in the whole rest of my life. And it was all on account of him and that Kentson. Every lousy bit of it.

I still wasn't calmed down when Curtis tapped on the door and asked to be let in.

"Whata ya want?" I barked at him.

"Open the door," he said whispering. "It's only me."

I got up off the bed and flicked the button on the door knob and rolled back on the bed again, face into the wall.

"Lock it," I told him.

He never said anything first. He went over to his desk and I spose he took out a book and started to read.

After about ten minutes he spoke to me.

"I told you to watch what you said to him."

"Ah, shut up!" I snapped. I wasn't in any mood for that.

He didn't answer me. He went back to whatever it was he was doing. Then, after another long spell of quiet, he said, "What are you going to do now, Mike?"

"None of your business."

I was pissed off still. But after a long time lying there and thinking about it, I knew there was no reason to be taking it out on him. I turned over and sat up on the bed, my back up against the wall.

"What are you going to do now?"

"Get the frig outa here, that's what."

"What, go back home?" he said.

"Maybe."

"Dad won't let you."

"The hell with him."

"He won't, I know he won't. Especially after tonight."

"You think I cares about him? If I wants to take off, I'll take off. And he won't be stopping me."

Curtis looked hard at me. "What, just sneak off and not tell anybody?"

"Why not?"

"How will you get there?"

"Thumb rides, if I got to."

"All the way to Marten? What about you don't get picked up?"

"I'll stay there until I do."

"And what about it starts to rain or something?"

"Ay, what is this? A bloody quiz game or something? If I gets it in my mind to go then I'll do it one way or the other. Nobody is going to stop me."

He sat there thinking about that for a long time. Like doing something like that was too much for him to believe.

I dug out every cent of money I could find. All the dough in every pants pocket and every drawer. Dumped it all in the middle of the bed. I counted it out. With the ten bucks Aunt Flo sent me the week before, it all came to $30.42.

"That's enough to get me a damn good ways. I can get home a dozen times with that much."

Curtis hardly noticed what I was doing. When I said how much it was it didn't seem to register with him. He was thinking about something else.

"I wonder what I could sell if I really needed money?" I started to think. "My watch I guess."

"Michael?" he said.

"Yeah," I said, still thinking.

"What about if I go with you?"

If he had fired a shotgun through the ceiling, I wouldn't a turned my head any faster.

"Wha? You're kiddin?"

"No." He shook his head. "I really think I want to go with you."

That was a lot more than I could believe.

"You're not bluffin?"

"No."

"Really?"

"No. I'm sick of this place."

"Hold on," I said. I had to have time to get this straight. "You mean you'd just up and leave?"

"Yeah."

"You mean you wouldn't mind hitchhiking?"

"Rain or snow, I wouldn't care."

"What if we don't get picked up?"

"What is this—a quiz game or something?"

We both laughed.

Holy shit. You talk about. Cripes, he wanted to run away from home. He wanted to skin out just as bad as I did. I had a buddy, a real buddy. I really had someone to take off with. I couldn't let a chance like that go by.

We shook on it. That sounds dumb. Something like you'd see in a movie on T.V. But that's what we done. We got up and shook hands on it. We was going to skin out from St. Albert together.

* * *

In an hour we had it all figured out perfect. That night we would get everything ready. The next morning, Tuesday, Curtis would make out he was going off to school like usual, only he'd double back and I'd meet him with the stuff and we'd take off. No more to it than that. It would be almost a whole day before anyone would start to wonder where we was. That would be enough of a head start that they wouldn't have a chance of catching up with us.

After talking to Curtis about what stuff we could lay our hands on, I figured out a new plan. We wouldn't go to Marten right away. We'd spend the first few days off in the woods somewhere. That'd give the old man something to chew his fingernails about.

The hardest part was getting the stuff ready without making anyone suspicious of what we was doing. We needed sleeping bags, of course, and knapsacks. Curtis had said that he could come up with both of them. There was a load of that stuff stashed away in the basement. With the old man's dough you had all that whether you needed it or not. Red nylon knapsacks with the aluminum frames. They might a been used once. It was the kind I'd seen hitchhikers on the highway with. In that way they fitted in perfect. It wasn't the kind I was use to. Anyone around home who spent much time in the woods wouldn't have that kind. Too big. Too expensive.

The sleeping bags—down-filled, arctic ones. Nothing but the best. The old fellow never spared the money. Curtis said that his old man had it in his mind that they'd do a lot of camping and hiking last summer. It was a sudden brainwave he had. A lot of families was starting to do it. So he got every one of them fitted out. And then, after one night in a canvas tent, they chucked it all up. I couldn't imagine either one of them making much of a go of it in a canvas tent, the fuss that was kicked up when there was either bit of dirt in the house. I could just picture Aunt Ellen waking up on a rainy morning or trying to cook breakfast over an open fire. It wouldn't be the state, I knows.

The knapsacks and sleeping bags was better than anything I could a dreamed for. Curtis snuck it all up into the bedroom without them knowing anything about it. Through the basement door, then out around the house to the bedroom window, where I grabbed it and hauled it in.

Two or three times we had to stuff it all under the beds in a hurry when Aunt Ellen came banging at the door. First she was trying to get me to come out for something to eat. I said no. Finally she got Curtis to go out and bring in a sandwich for me. I wouldn't eat it, no way. Another time she came banging on the door because she said I was wanted on the phone. I sent Curtis out to see who it was.

It was Brenda.

The whole time since that morning Brenda

hardly came into my mind. After we started packing I thought of her once, how I should maybe try to see her before we took off. Then I forgot it again. I had too much other stuff on my mind to be thinking about girls.

Then her phone call. I sent Curtis back a second time, telling him to say to her that I couldn't come to the phone right away. I would get a hold of her tomorrow. Maybe I would be outside the school around dinnertime.

That was a lie, of course. I wouldn't see her the next day. Perhaps I'd never see her again. For a while that bugged me. Then again the idea of sticking around just to be near her was foolish. I liked her a lot. I really did. But it couldn't a been love, now could it?

I would write her a letter. That's what came in my mind to do. Write a letter and explain everything. I did that later on, after all the packing was finished and everything was all set for the next day. The two pages I wrote wouldn't get any prize for the best letter ever written to a girl, but it wasn't bad, if I have to say so myself.

I knew that Brenda was probably feeling really rotten about the whole thing, blaming herself for all that happened. So I started off by telling her that Kentson had no cause to go shooting off his big mouth like he done, no matter what. Then I figured I better set her straight about everything else that went on that day, because who knows what garbage other people had been trying to tell her. But the bit about where we planned to go—I didn't trust even her with much information about that.

I ended up the letter with a part about how much I would miss her. It was tough to get it down the way I wanted it. But after enough times, I got it right.

I sealed up the envelope and put it on the desk right out in front so I wouldn't forget to mail it in the morning. Then I got ready for bed. I got in under the covers, turned off the light, but I didn't go to sleep. I stayed awake till I was sure everyone else in the house was in bed and asleep. Then I unlocked the door quietly and looked out. I tip-toed to the bathroom. You can just imagine what a relief that was. After all that time, I needed a leak so bad that it felt like my top teeth was floating.

PART THREE

15

The morning plan went off like clockwork. Not a hitch. Like he always done, the army sergeant rapped his knuckles on the door at seven-thirty. He spit out a little reminder about me apologizing to the Kentsons, "or when I get home from work I'll drag you over there myself."

I wouldn't even let him know I was awake. By the time you gets home from work, I had a mind to tell him, I'll be long gone. Then you'll have something else to yell about.

Our setup came off like this:

> 8:30—Curtis strolled out of the house. Shouted to his mother that he wouldn't be home till late in the afternoon. Said he had a chess club meeting.
> 8:31—The drop-off of the knapsacks from the bedroom window in plastic garbage bags.
> 8:32—Curtis laid down the two garbage bags near the side of the house and went on walking down the street.

8:50—I came out of the bedroom and told Aunt Ellen that I wasn't hungry. Didn't say much else to her except that I was going for a walk and if I didn't get back to dinner it was because I might go over to the hospital after to spend some time there. Yes, I had money enough to buy dinner.

8:53—Put on my heavy work boots and my winter coat. Exit from the house.

8:55—The two garbage bags in my hands, I proceeded down the street. No problems. I was carrying the strong ones.

9:01—Crossed paths with Curtis near Kelly's. Everything fine. Fingers crossed, no fool-up yet.

Then our biggest, toughest decision of all morning—what to do with the stupid math book Curtis was sposed to be carrying to school.

"Fire the thing in the garbage can, you dummy. Do something with it," I told him. "Com' on."

Now, if you're Curtis, one thing you don't do is fire books in garbage cans. First he had it in his mind to take it with him until I talked him outa that. No sir, nothing like that gets taken with us. Then he was going to ask the girl who worked in the drugstore to hold on to it for him, the stun arse. Finally, you know what he went to work and done? He got fifty cents worth of stamps from the stamp machine next to the mailbox, licked the whole works the one time, and flattened them all on the outside cover of the book. He wrote his address on the inside. Then he let her slide, down into the mailbox on top of my letter to Brenda. Can you picture that? Cripes, I just about died laughing at him.

Then we started walking to the highway. Each of us had a garbage bag in our hand. By ten o'clock we was on the shoulder of the road, knapsacks on the backs, thumbs out. Within fifteen minutes we had our first ride. Ay, on our way!

It was that easy. No sweat atall, my son. We'd be long gone, Teddy boy, by the time you got smart enough to figure out what happened.

"Where're you fellows goin this time of the day? Aren't you supposed to be in school?" The words coming from the driver of this Chevy Nova that picked us up. After, that is, we was aboard the car with the door closed and driving off.

Well, we was bound to strike a few little snags. But no problems that I couldn't handle. That was minor stuff.

"No, we got a holiday. Trouble with the furnace," I said right away, real quick on the answers.

I sure could crack them off when I had the need to. Probably the school had electric heat, for all I knew. The school home was shut down three times in one month last year with furnace trouble. So I figured it would be as good a thing to say as any.

"How far are you goin?" I asked him. All the time completely relaxed, you know.

"Oh, it's about seventy miles, I guess."

I gave Curtis a little wink with the old eye there. Not bad for the first ride. Not bad atall. Now I'm no pro when it comes to thumbing rides. Home I was all the time hitching a ride back and forth between Marten and the next place down along the shore, Spencer's Harbour. But that's only four miles. And I knew practically everyone who had a car anyway. Even though Mom wasn't very fussy about me doing it.

Well, anyway, we was going along great, enjoying the ride, you knows, like you would. Thinking to myself—this is it, I'm actually leaving St. Albert behind. Heavens only knows where we might end up, but what odds. Every mile was one mile farther away from misery.

Hard to say what was going on in Curtis' mind back in the back seat. He was the one who wanted to come. Nobody forced him into it. Maybe he had the same relief I did. Who knows.

Anyway, we was going along great when buddy started pumping the holy load of questions to us. He was an old fellow, I spose around sixty-five. One of those fellows who wants to know everything. And I was the one who had to come up with all the answers. No way would Curtis open his mouth.

Well, I laid it on—this fancy big string of lies about a mile long. All about how we was brothers and we was going to Gander to visit our sister who lived there with her two children, Susan and Craig—I put names on them right there on the spot. And how since the school was closed to put in a new furnace, we'd be able to spend all that time at our sister's place. And how she loved to see us come.

And nah, our parents didn't mind us hitchhiking like this, not atall, because it saved so much money with bus fares gone up now, and nah, there was no danger to it anyway since we'd done it thousands of times before. We wasn't scared of getting stuck without a ride because people always picked up young fellows our age. They felt sorry for us. And no, never once in all the times we done it, did we ever get stuck out on the highway in the cold and the rain. We always listened to the forecast before we left. That's one thing our parents always done was make sure it wasn't going to rain or snow. No, it had to be a good forecast right across the island before they'd think about letting us go.

You knows I didn't crack them off. All that was just flowing outa me. Not only that, but once I got started, it got easier and easier. Like I was a born liar. Well, I had to do something to keep the old fellow happy. He was firing questions left and right sir, like half the reason he picked us up was to get our life story.

He wasn't too bad of a fellow all around, I spose. It was just that he asked so many bloody questions. He had me kept going all the time trying to come up with answers. Then he says, "Your brother doesn't say much, does he?"

"Nah, he's got trouble with hes ears. He's practically deaf. He's in a bad state. You might gab on and on to en all day long and he won't give any heed to a word you says. Doctor says he might be completely deaf in three of four years. Not a thing they can do for en." I winked at Curtis.

"God, that's too bad," the fellow says. And he says it so much like he means it, like it came right straight from his heart, that all of a sudden I figured I should never a told him that.

The strangest kind of feeling started to come over me. I started to get mad at myself and ashamed that I lied like a real son-of-a-bitch to the old fellow the way I done. And when I was doing it I was getting the biggest kinda kick out of it too. That made it worse. And I didn't just stop at a few lies to answer his questions, I went on and on cracking off the big ones and him believing it like it was the gospel truth.

I tell you I didn't know what was getting into me.

Guilt like that might seem stupid. Probably I'd never lay eyes on the old fellow again. But here I was making him feel sorry for us when he might a had all kinds of trouble of his own. His wife might a been real sick or something, for God's sake. And for no reason atall, I gave him something else to get himself upset over. I felt guilty as hell. I never lied as bad as that before. And shit, it was starting to louse up everything on the very first day.

I was more than glad when he finally stopped

the car and we got out. I said thank you, but I
couldn't look him straight in the face. To top it
all off, he told me to take real good care of my
brother and then he took five dollars out of his
wallet to give me so's I could get a good cap to
cover Curtis' ears in case it got cold, he said.

The way he said it made me think of Aunt Flo.
That's just like something Aunt Flo would do. And
Aunt Flo is such a kind old person that I felt like
a piece of dirt when buddy said it.

I told him no thank you very much sir but it is
very nice of you. He'll be okay. And closed the
door real quick.

See, I can certainly screw up things for myself.
I made a vow then and there that if there was
any more lies that I'd have to tell then they'd only
be enough to get us off the hook. That was all.
Not a word more.

Seeing as we got so far on the first ride, I
thought maybe we wouldn't need to go back at it
with the thumbs right away, that we could probably spare a few minutes to get something to eat.
By this time, where I had gone for so long without
anything in my stomach, I was ready to tackle
just about the first thing we came across in the
way of food. We found a store and laid into the
bars and drinks, and a bunch of the best-looking
bananas I could ever a hoped to find. I loves
bananas. I can eat bananas till the whites of my
eyes turns yellow. By the time we made it back

to the highway we had practically the whole works of them devoured.

"Curtis," I said, "you got to do some talkin this time, buddy."

"I don't know what to say."

"Well, say something. Anything. I don't care what it is. But don't just sit there like a dummy."

"I'll try."

God, some try all right. He might a said three words the whole time we was with the next guy that picked us up.

I didn't mind it too much just the same. Because it turned out that the fellow was a wildlife officer and we had her made for things to talk about. When he hauled over to the side of the road I could see four quarters and the head of a moose lying there in the back of the pickup. I figured the moose must a been poached or struck on the highway with a car or something. I couldn't figure what else it could be.

The fellow driving was in a uniform, but he was only a young fellow and he was a great one to have a chat with. We talked practically the whole way to Grand Falls. It turned out I was right—the moose was hit by a car. Killed the moose and demolished the car. Bad way for a moose to go.

A fine year on moose, the fellow said. Lots of hunters got their moose this year. Then I remembered that this was the fall I was sposed to go with Dad when he went on his hunting trip. We would a had our moose too, cause Dad knew right where to go.

I've seen a good many moose other times when we've been driving along the highway. And I came up on one once in the woods when I was in setting slips, but I never been out and been there when one was shot. I thought for a while that I wouldn't want to be at it, because the moose is such a nice-looking animal when you sees one running through the woods. But I figured that if there's a lot of them on the go and the meat could be put to good use, then I wouldn't mind doing it. I snares rabbits and kills them. Sure it's the same thing.

When we got into Grand Falls, the fellow let us off there just after he turned down at the traffic lights. Even though it's the Trans-Canada, they still got traffic lights in the middle of it. Think they'd have an overpass or something seeing it's the Trans-Canada. We got out and I said thank you and that I certainly enjoyed the ride. Hope we'd be lucky enough to get another one like that.

"Good-bye," Curtis said. That made it four words. I had to laugh at that fellow.

We took the knapsacks and put them on our backs and then we walked for maybe a mile and a half to get away from the stores and garages, and out to where it looked more like a highway.

It must a been half an hour this time before anyone stopped to pick us up. Still we was making pretty good time. It was about two o'clock. Good time, that is, up till then. I was a bit scared all along that we wouldn't make it before dark to where I had it in mind to go. It was okay though, the way it worked out, because we ended up spending the night in Gander airport.

If you ever gets your hands on a map you'll see that Grand Falls and Gander are about sixty miles apart. One has a big newsprint mill (and a stink of sulphur) and the other is pretty well known for its airport. It gets a lot of overseas flights that stops for fuel, flying back and forth from Europe.

With any half-decent driver it shouldn't a took us more than an hour to make it to Gander from where we got picked up. But the thing was, we didn't have a half-decent driver. The third one to stop for us was a woman. The slowest kind. Not only that, but she was driving a Volkswagen beetle. Now, small cars like that is not exactly something that gets me excited, to put it mildly. If I had a choice between one of them and a bicycle, I'd have to think twice about the bicycle.

I shouldn't complain I spose. Because she did stop and buy us a load of grub. Just about ten bucks worth. See, when I let on that I didn't have all that much to eat since the day before, she just about had a canary. Old women are forever doing that to me, stuffing me with food. I guess it makes them feel good. Like a mother or something.

She stopped in at this Irving Restaurant on the highway and ordered up two big hot turkey sandwiches. And the biggest glasses of milk she could get. She sat across from us then in the booth with a bowl of soup and watched us stuff our faces. Not saying we didn't make short work of the food, because we certainly did. Me especially. It was the first real meal I had since breakfast the day before. The old gut was just about caved in.

That really knocked me out that did. Her buying those big platefuls of grub for us and then having a measly little bowl of soup herself. For dessert then she lets us have a sundae each and orders us two pieces of pie besides. Lord dyin, I wouldn't want to see us if we was related to her. We'd be just like the pigs.

We walked outa the restaurant blowed right up to the two eyeballs. To tell the truth, I can't see why she done it. I mean, we might a looked pitiful, but we couldn't a looked *that* pitiful. Besides, she never seen us before in her life. I spose she's just one of those who makes a habit of going out of their way to do good turns for people. Lots still around like that.

I bet you anything she would a had us into her house for a cup of tea and a few buns if it had been home where she was headed. But she was on her way to Gander to catch a plane to England somewhere to see her daughter. As it was I had to tell her about ten times that the sister we had in Gander was sure to be home and that she really was expecting us.

She was going to drive us right to the door of the house till I told her I couldn't remember the street and what we always done was to go to the airport and phone our sister and she'd come and pick us up. It didn't sound so hot saying I didn't know the street after just telling her not five minutes before that we'd been there a thousand times. I had to sorta slip over that fast. I made up this fake telephone number right quick like—674-0891. Then she told me she was sure all Gander phone numbers began with 256.

Frig, you're not stun either. I was getting worse. Well, I said to her, I'll check it out in the phone book. Maybe that was the number of my uncle in Halifax. I spose to God she didn't know the Halifax numbers too.

What sorta convinced her was seeing me in the airport using the phone. From the line-up at the Air Canada counter she couldn't see that I didn't even put in any money. Thank God her plane was due to leave in half an hour. She would a had us mesmerized, making sure we was all right.

We had this big thank-you scene. Cripes, I thought for a minute she was going to kiss us both on the cheeks. I'm forever getting mixed up with these older mothers or aunts or something who wants to kiss me. That's the truth, I am. Natural beauty I spose.

As she was going in to get checked past the security guard and into the waiting room, I yelled out to her that I thought my sister was coming now and be sure to have a good time in England. I said that to make her feel good. For a laugh, I almost bawled out, "and dress warm," like they always do to me when I goes anywhere. Only I didn't do it. I thought it might spoil things.

I got to stop right here and go back a bit. See, there's one little matter about our meeting up with this woman, Mrs. McKay, that I haven't got around to mentioning yet. It was pretty important to everything that happened afterwards.

I arranged it so that we could steal her car.

Okay, okay. That's a bit much as far as the cops is concerned. I knows that. Me being only fourteen and not having a licence. But what else could I do?

See, the whole way from Grand Falls all I could think about was—now sposing we *do* end up getting a ride right to the place where we wants to go. What is the fellow going to think of letting us off there? Plus, once word got out that we was missing, the first thing the fellow is going to do is report to the cops that he picked up two young fellows and let them off at such-an-such a place. Then the cops would be right there to grab us.

I kept thinking what the hell are we going to do to get over that problem. Then it came to me. If we had a car or a motorcycle or something we could drive it there ourselves and nobody'd have any trace at all of us to follow.

A car? The old woman's Volkswagen of course. The perfect situation. She gone to England for two weeks. She wouldn't have to know a thing about it. I likes to think we borrowed the car, not stole it atall.

Of course the problem was how to get the thing without her knowing. Well, the way I done it, it couldn't a worked out any better. See, she was in the airport, right, waiting to get herself checked in. I came back from the phone booth and told her that I got through to my sister and that she would be down in a little while, as soon as her husband came back from the grocery store. Then, with her still in line, I told her all of a sudden that I left my gloves in the car and could I please have the keys so I could run out and get them.

I really did leave my gloves in the car. Right under the front seat where I stuffed them. So I ran back out just like the lightning after she dug the keys up out of her purse.

When I felt the ring of about ten keys in my hand, my mind kissed her fair and square on the lips. I thought maybe she'd have another set with one or two on the chain. And then I would never a been able to take one without her noticing it. I would a had to hot wire the car or something later on. But with all those keys she'd never miss one unless she took the trouble to look real close. That was a chance I figured I had to take.

Out at the car I found the right key to open the door, checked to make sure that it was the same one that fit the ignition, and then put it into my pocket. I took out my gloves. I left one door open too, just in case.

On my way back I stopped at the end of the airport building to see if I could see what she was doing before I went up to her with the keys. She was still at the counter. Perfect. I walked up fast, with the gloves sorta waving in the air a bit. Handed her the keys then as she was talking to the guy about her ticket. She shoved them in her purse without even blinking an eyelid.

She asked me later if I made sure the doors was locked. I didn't want to, but I had no choice, I had to lie.

I knows all this sounds like out and out stealing. Come right down to it and it was. But to me, like I said, it was almost like borrowing some fellow's bike. I only wanted it for a couple of days. It wouldn't get hurt. Nobody would know the difference.

When her flight finally left the ground, I was some relieved. I half expected her to come running back after she got checked past security, waving around a set of keys and saying there was one missing. But she didn't. She got into the air and I never seen the woman again.

Well, old Curtis didn't know a thing about all this. He didn't have a clue about what I'd gone and done. I figured if it was going to be done atall, then only one person was going to do it anyway. So what was the use of telling him beforehand. The only thing he might a done was loused it up.

That knocked him over altogether that did—when I told him we had a car and we was going for a little drive in the morning. He didn't know what to say to that.

Cool or what?

16

By the time Mrs. McKay's flight had gone it was four-thirty. That was three o'clock in New York, three o'clock in Montreal, and eight o'clock in London, England, according to the clocks on the terminal wall. It would a been all right for us if we was in Montreal or New York. We'd a had an hour and a half more of daylight. But where we was, with it being November and the times gone back the week before, it was already pretty close to getting dark. That put the clamps right there on the idea of making the last part of the trip that first day. I wasn't about to take a chance on going off with the car in the dark. There might be enough trouble with her in the daylight, let alone when it got pitch black.

I didn't mind that so much anyway, as long as the extra few hours didn't fool us up for the next day. I wasn't sure how long it was going to take before the cops everywhere would get a hold of the fact that we was missing and be on the lookout for us.

We'd just have to chance it. We'd spend the night where we was and get an early start in the morning. The airport building was big enough to get lost into and I knew for a fact that it was open all night. I figured we could stretch out on one of the seats somewhere later on and snooze her off. There was plenty of them there.

That was for later. To kill the next few hours, we decided we'd leave the airport and go out to town—roam around a bit, see what there was to see. We stowed away the knapsacks in the car and took off then and walked the mile or so to the shopping centre. We had some shopping to do— not much, some food and camping supplies to pick up for the next few days. Then we bummed around for a while until I figured we'd better get outa sight and go to a movie or something. I had this crazy feeling that if we walked around too much someone might just happen to recognize us. I mean, I was only ever in the place once before in my life. But still, Newfoundland don't have that many people. You never knows when a relative or someone that you met before is going to pop up outa nowhere. Don't kid yourself. I've seen it happen.

By ten o'clock we was back to the airport. We took the knapsacks from the car and brought them into the terminal again. That way we looked at least like we had some right to be there.

The centre area in the terminal must be about the biggest waiting room I ever sat down into. It can't be much, say, compared to Montreal or Toronto or something, but it's still pretty big. They got seventy-five of these long padded lounge chairs, I counted them. They're not meant for sleeping on, but I mean you could sleep a darn fine crowd of people there if they was ever stuck for a place to take a nap.

Something else that'll give you an idea of the size of the place is the men's washroom. It's got seven urinals in it. Now, I don't make a job of counting everything around, but when you're standing up there and you got nothing better to do, well then you might as well be at that as at anything. As far as the eye can see—all these places to take a leak.

Now that's what I calls fair-size accommodations. We could a slept in the car, I spose, but it was cold outside and even with the sleeping bags we wouldn't a been very comfortable the way we would a had to be squat up. Anyway, you'd think in a place that size they wouldn't mind a coupla fellows spending the night there. After all, it wasn't as if the place was crowded. Even when the planes was in, there was thousands of room for everybody who wanted to sit down, and loads left over.

But sure enough, just like I should've expected, about one o'clock in the night, between flights when there was hardly a soul around and just as we was settled away comfortable, the darn security guard jams on the brakes right next to us and gives us each a bloody big shake. Just about landed me on the floor. I had a mind to draw off and belt him one.

Now, see, if I'd been someone else, older and all dressed up in a shirt and tie and with three pieces of luggage and a briefcase, he wouldn't a batted an eye. I bet you he wouldn't've.

I told him we was waiting to get on the CN bus in the morning. I had to say something. For sure Curtis wasn't going to deliver a speech to him. I couldn't say we was waiting for a flight cause he would a asked for our tickets. And see with the CN bus we could a been buying our tickets the next morning. The ticket office wasn't open until then.

So I thought that was a pretty good answer. Only he didn't swallow it so good. Seems like someone might a tried that before.

"What are you doin here all night, when the bus doesn't leave until one o'clock tomorrow?"

So I had to make up this story about how we lived in this place a long ways away that wasn't on the bus line and Gander was the closest place that the bus stopped and we only had this one chance for a ride in and that was last evening with another fellow because Dad was away in the woods and he wasn't there to drive us. We was on our way to St. John's to see our sister.

He still wasn't so sure. But finally, he came out with one of those okay-but-remember lectures and walked off. Wouldn't know but we was trying to wreck the place. Cripes, we spent a coupla bucks in the gift shop there. What more did he want? We was good for business.

By nine o'clock the next day, close to twenty-four hours from the time we left St. Albert, we made it to our temporary hide-out in the woods.

I've been driving a pickup now since I've been ten years old. That's no lie. Where we lived in Marten we had a nice-size section of cleared land out in back of the house where we raised our vegetables. That's mainly where I learned to drive. Back and forth the driveway and up over the hill and around the land. And then too, lots of times when I was with Dad anywhere in the pickup off from the main road, he'd let me take the wheel. Not all that far now, because you had to be careful of the cops.

Some fathers wouldn't let anybody that age go near a steering wheel. Dad wasn't like that. He said I had to learn sometime and it was all right I got use to it early. As long as I didn't keep on after him all the time to be going places then he didn't mind. It wasn't dangerous because there was no traffic where we use to go. And anyway I knew what I was doing. I took my time. Sunday afternoons mostly, after Dad had his nap, was when we'd be out.

I'll have to admit that a Volkswagen was a bit different from what I was use to. But not a big lot. What I done first was to lodge a couple of coats under my behind until I was a good comfortable distance above the wheel. I hauled on an old beanie over my head that I found in one of the coat pockets and covered half my face with a pair of Mrs. McKay's sunglasses that Curtis dug out from the glove compartment. I turned down the sun visor.

"All you need is a white scarf and you'll be ready to fly," Curtis said.

Well, you knows he didn't come up with it. I felt like giving him a good bang. Me trying to be serious and him fooling around like that. He was supposed to be keeping a lookout and telling me what was going on around the parking lot.

I took me a while to get her around the pile of cars that was there and then onto the road. Longer than I figured. There was a few little extra stops and starts I hadn't counted on. But once I made it out and got to the straight stretches and had a chance to get use to the way she handled, then there wasn't much to it atall. It was all a matter of being careful, of taking it slow and easy.

It was so early in the morning when we started that there was hardly any traffic on the go. That was one good thing. Our biggest problem was getting gas. I knew the tank didn't have enough in it to get us there and back. And we certainly couldn't take the risk of driving her to empty. We turned in real quick to a self-service place and gassed her up fast is what we done. I stayed aboard the car and made out I was fixing something under the dash. The girl inside never got all that much of a look at me. Curtis went out to

the pumps and put in three dollars worth and paid
the girl and came running back out just as I
popped my head up.

"Flatten her!" he said.

Now that's how much he knew about it. Good
thing I was the one driving. I played it cool and
drove out quietly. I don't figure she caught on.

With that problem behind us, our other head-
ache was coming up against the cops. That was
the main reason for leaving so early. There was
less chance of meeting them. We was lucky too
that the fifty miles we had to go didn't take us
through either community. It was all woods but
for three or four gas stations.

Anyway, we made it, like I said. And we didn't
see not one cop car along the way. I drove about
forty-five most of the time, about seventy if you
wants to talk kilometres. She had a fair bit of
power, I spose, but I mean I had to keep my head
and play it safe. I couldn't mat her my first time
driving on the highway and all. I had to be
sensible about it. Wreck the car and then what
kinda shit would we a been in.

It was just a few minutes before nine when we
hauled into our destination—the overflow campground in the National Park. Even before we left
the house, when I was trying to come up with a
good place to hide out for a few days, this campground popped right into my mind. I was there
with the family two summers before when we

went on a week's camping trip. I remembered it because it had shelters and running water and indoor toilets and electricity and all that stuff, which made living there not the least bit like camping.

The running water and the power might be cut off but I knew the shelters had to be still there and that was what we needed—a place to give us some shelter from the weather. If worse came to worse we still had the car to fall back on. Although I tell you the idea of being cramped up for fourteen hours a day like two sardines wasn't much to look forward to.

The plan now was to spend a few days in the park and then skin out to Marten after that, once we'd proved to those guys that we could get along good enough without them. When the time came and we decided we was ready to leave, we'd drive back to the airport with the car, then thumb the hundred miles home to Marten.

We drove down the branch road from the highway and then turned up the road with the arrow for the campground. The building for checking in campers and the parking lot both was hard to see from the main road. They was hidden in behind some trees. Perfect.

There was a chain across the road to the campsites with a sign saying CLOSED/FERME. Not so perfect.

But then again, it meant for sure nobody was going into the place. The sign in the window of the building said CAMPGROUND CLOSED, PROCEED TO WINTER CAMPING AREA 12 MILES EAST.

So what if we couldn't drive up to it. I parked the car there by the building. That was good enough, nobody would ever see it from the main road. We got out, jumped over the chain, and ran off up the road to get a first-hand look at the whole thing. We came running in on what looked to me like a place that hadn't seen a trace of human life in weeks. Maybe months. There was all kinds of signs up like I remembered them, saying sites 26 to 38 that way, 52 to 59 another way, where to go to use the can, the forest-fire index is low, that way for the playground, drive with caution. All that. Like I said, no more like camping out in the woods now than camping in the middle of Yonge Street in Toronto. But for what I was after this time, it was just the thing.

I spose if we had scouted around the whole place we would a come across probably two hundred of these sites, each of them with a picnic table, a fireplace, and some kind of level spot to pitch a tent or haul in a camper trailer.

We took a quick look at the cooking shelters and the washrooms. It never came into my mind before about the washrooms for a place to sleep. Two of them was locked up, but number three— that one was open. We could a made do with the cooking shelters. They had a roof, a floor, and full walls up three sides. But now then, the washroom was a regular Holiday Inn. Once you was inside, not a bit of weather could get at you, not if it was buried in ten foot of snow.

Okay, so a can might seem a pretty lousy place to use for sleeping, but I'm telling you, with this place we'd have solid comfort. And anyway it wasn't actually the washroom part we was going to sleep in, it was the janitor's storeroom that joined up the men's can to the women's on the the other side.

That put us on easy street. A place off by ourselves away from everybody. Lots of room. All kinds of shelter—from rain, snow, hail, sleet, whatever you mind to name. No running water now. That was shut off for the winter. We'd have to make do with water from a pond or spring. Just terrible idn't it what you got to put up with when you're camping? I mean no electricity and no T.V. either! Can't see how we'd ever survive!

And grub? Well, we had a few things brought with us. Enough to keep off starvation. But mostly I was counting on the coil of wire I had in my pocket to do the trick. In a place like that there had to be thousands of rabbits, and maybe some partridge. No hunting in the national parks—that was the law, of course. Ah, but the federal government would never miss a coupla rabbits, I thought. They'd only die off anyway in a few years. And what use would they be to anybody then. Besides, I was sure the government didn't want to see us go hungry. I called it a kind of government grant for the needy.

So we was all set, all fixed away nice. I felt pretty darn happy about how things had worked out. We could count ourselves awful lucky. And Curtis, what did he think about it all? My son, once he knew he had a bit of security as far as a half-decent place to sleep was concerned, that was it then, he didn't give a darn.

"Shit, old man, this is goin to be all right."

The dumb nut was starting to sound like me.

Later on we got straightened away and had something to eat. Vienna sausages in the blue cans—the old stand-by. But then no kettle for the tea. We had to do something about that. I couldn't find not one thing to use, so we ended up eating a full can of peaches so I could take the can and make a kettle out of it. Had to open it with a pocket knife too. Might a known we wouldn't think of buying something simple like a can opener. Then I fixed it up with a piece of rabbit wire. Out with the tea bags and of course no water. It was half an hour before we found a brook and got back with some water. But we had our tea. No sense being in the woods and not having tea. Can drinks and junk is all right for a picnic, but to make it either bit like you're really in the woods, then you gotta have the tea.

There was nothing like it. Tea in the woods

somehow tastes ten times better, anyway. The two of us having a mugup by the open fire, the air a bit cold and frosty, us being on our own. All of it put together, it made me feel right on top of the world.

17

I guess Curtis did pick up a few things about catching rabbits. I tried to teach him a bit as I went along. It meant starting right from scratch. I doubt if he ever seen a piece of rabbit wire before in his life, or what a good rabbit's path looked like, that kinda thing. The first slip I set out, I asked him to go cut me a standard—a stick to tie the slip onto—and he comes back with an old dead stick, old man, that wouldn't hold a shrew, let alone a rabbit squirming all he was worth to save his neck. I tried not to laugh, but I had to.

After he watched me set out a few, I found a good path for him and let him tail one himself. I had to fix it over; he had it too low to the ground and too small a loop for the time of the year it was, but other than that he done pretty good for the first time.

I had a great time, myself. It really felt good to be back at it like that. Only thing was I missed Dad. When I thought about it after, I knew then that was the main reason I didn't have very much patience with Curtis. I was thinking too much about Dad. What I wouldn't a give for him to a been there. But I didn't let it play on my mind too much, because I knew what would a happened if I did.

That first day in the campground was the fifth of November. In Newfoundland that means Bonfire Night. Or Guy Fawkes Night, whatever you mind to call it. It's the anniversary of the time he tried to burn down the English Parliament in the 1600's. I think that Newfoundland is about the only place in North America that celebrates it anymore. See, it wasn't so long ago that we was a colony of Britain.

I couldn't let November fifth pass and not have a bonfire, no way. Me and Curtis lit a small one just as it was getting dark, there in one of the campsites. We had to keep it small and then dout it before it got too dark because we couldn't take any chances on cars seeing it from the road. If they seen flankers coming up through the trees someone might just run up thinking it was a forest fire or something.

It wasn't much like what I was use to. Pitiful, it was. If I'd been home we'd a had some fire. Last year the one me and the boys had was the biggest of all the fires in Marten, and there must a been at least twenty or more around the place. We cut boughs for a week after school and we collected up about a hundred car tires and throwed in along with that. Nothing pitiful about that fire. You couldn't get within not ten foot of it, it was giving off so much heat.

There I had to settle for a lousy little campground fire. And where it got dark so early, we was all finished with it before supper.

We dug out something to eat, and then we fooled around and played cards till about nine o'clock. With the power shut off, it was a good thing we'd brought candles. And there's nothing either like living next door to two useless cans.

We squirmed down into the sleeping bags then, and blew out the light. We shot the bull in the dark and thought about trying to get to sleep. It was going to be a frosty night, a good one on rabbits. And, I was hoping, a good one for us too. By six o'clock in the morning we'd know if the sleeping bags was as good as they was cracked up to be. I knew how cold it would get by that time.

We really should a been good and sleepy. We'd been on the go a lot the last coupla days and what with the security guard snooping around the night before, we didn't get much of a rest. We should a flaked out right away. But, no way sir. We was almost as wide awake as we'd been all day.

In the dark, I wondered just how brave Curtis was about the whole thing now. Maybe he had some second thoughts about running away?

"Scared?" I said, trying to root something outa him.

"Shit no," he said, as fast as that.

I spose I had to believe him. Even though it was black as tar in the room (there was not a window anywhere in the whole place), there was nothing really to be frightened of.

Curtis had turned on the transistor radio I brought with me. I had stuffed it into my knapsack the last minute before we left. We was listening some of the time to the top ten, but what we was really waiting for was the two minutes of news every hour. Sure enough, we made it to the ten o'clock news.

"There is still no word on the whereabouts of the two fourteen-year-old boys missing since yesterday morning from their home in St. Albert. Officials of the RCMP, however, indicate that they have received two separate reports from drivers who have picked up boys meeting their description hitchhiking east on the Trans-Canada. One driver reported to police that he had let off two boys in the Grand Falls area at approximately one-thirty p.m. yesterday, but no further reports on their possible whereabouts have yet been received. Anyone travelling in the Grand Falls area recently who may have information helpful in locating these boys is asked to contact the nearest detachment of the RCMP."

So. We had the Mounties on our tails. Like I thought. We was safe enough, though. Mrs. Mc-Kay was in England now, and they had no trace of us past Grand Falls. Unless, of course, the security guard at the terminal got smart. Even then, he didn't have a clue where we might a gone.

"You worried?"

"Shit no," again.

"They haven't got one clue about where we are, not one. We could be in South America for all anybody knows."

"Let em suffer."

That's what we was doing all right, letting them suffer. Especially Curtis' old man. Good enough for him. He deserved to suffer for a change. Find out what it's like to be getting the dirty end of the stick. Having to take it now instead of dishing it out. That'll make the old man think twice. Make him learn the hard way that this stupid yelling and roughing up don't work all the time.

And then I started thinking—who was I to be talking? A fellow who lied black and blue and stole somebody else's car. I might as well a said it—"stole." That started playing on my mind. The sooner I could get it back on the parking lot the better. Only we couldn't do it right away or we'd mess everything up.

What the hell, I said to myself, forget about that for now. We're here away from everyone like we wanted, and we're darn well not going to let anything stop us from enjoying ourselves.

"Whata we goin at tomorrow?" I said to get myself thinking about something different. There was no need to talk very loud. The room was pretty narrow. We was right next to each other in the sleeping bags.

"We'll look at the slips."

"Maybe we'll set out a few more. And have a bloody big feed on all the rabbits we're going to get."

"Right on, man," he said.

"Now you're talkin.'"

"You got it."

"We're all set."

"Right you are."

"Proper t'ing."

"Proper t'ing. Proper t'ing. Proper t'ing."

And I turned over laughing, snuggled down in the sleeping bag, and went to sleep.

When we woke up the next morning everything outside was white with snow. I stopped the door open with a broom handle to let in some light, and got back in the sleeping bag where it was warm. I guess the sleeping bags had proved to be what they was cracked up to be, all right.

It couldn't a been much below freezing outside, but the snow was dribbling down in big, wet flakes. It was a beautiful sight to see.

"It looks awful nice, but it's screwing up our chances for a rabbit, unless one got in before it come to snow."

Curtis took one look outside through his half-opened eyes and then sunk back down in the sleeping bag and covered up his head.

I shouted at him, "I said, this ain't so good for rabbits, this kinda weather. It covers in the slips."

He didn't move an inch.

I could a let him stay there I spose. There was no real reason for him to be getting up yet. It was just that I was wide awake. And all this cold wet stuff outside and him so comfortable and me looking for a bit of fun. Well, it looked like it could be a laugh.

I eased up off my back and leaned out through the door still in the sleeping bag, and grabbed up a small bit of snow and packed it together tight. I laid back on the floor again and real quick like I shoved it down through the top of the sleeping bag onto the bare part of his neck.

You talk about the roar! He jumped about ten feet.

"You frigger!" he yelled, squirming around like mad to try to get the snow out. "You frigger!"

He hauled off and belted me with his arm. I jumped outa the sleeping bag and then on top of him, and that turned it right into a full-scale wrestling match.

In the coupla months we'd known each other, we never once wrestled or anything. We never joked around and had a few cracks at each other like you'd think two fellows living in the same room might. Curtis was never the kind of fellow who you carried on with like that.

Thirty seconds wrestling with him and there was no trouble to see why. It only proved to me what I knew all along—that there wasn't much on him anywhere that could pass for muscle, even if you stretched the truth.

"Now, whata ya goin to do?" I had him pinned to the floor, one knee on each of his arms and me sitting on his gut.

"Get off me, you ape!"

"What can ya do about it?"

He twisted and turned, kicked and shoved, but he couldn't budge me. All it done was move him closer to the door. I reached out through and got some more snow. I held it up in my hand above his face and sprinkled it down on top of him. He jerked his head from side to side, and tried to spit it back at me.

Up to then it was pretty much all fun. But he didn't get off on this new game too well. So I stopped it and then let him throw me over. I mean I could a kept him there all day like that if I'd wanted to. Only I figured it would be better if I let him have a chance back at me. Just because we was friends, that was all.

He struggled and struggled as hard as he could and I didn't even work up a sweat. We tumbled back and forth over the floor. A few times till he thought he had me, only then I got serious and sent him flying back on his arse in one quick move.

But he was determined to get revenge some-how. He ran out of doors just like he was and grabbed a full handful of snow and fired it in at me. Only I ducked and he missed.

He had a shirt and pants on because he'd figured it might be cold in the sleeping bag during the night, but he had nothing on his feet. Him barefoot in all that snow, pelting it in at me.

At least I had socks on. But no shirt, because I'm no good for sleeping with a shirt on, unless it gets really cold. I managed to dodge the first couple, but then he got lucky and started getting in a few hits on the bare back, so I took off out the door after him, snow or no snow.

He ran off across the road, what you'd call pretty nifty, because there was rocks and sticks under it all. And like a stun arse I was right behind him, scooping up what snow I could as I ran. Getting a few good smacks at him with it too.

Cripes, we ran the whole way, right around the string of campsites. Knows it wasn't nar bit chilly! Cold enough to freeze your nuts off. One fellow in his bare feet, the other one with a pair of socks and pants on but no shirt or nothing.

We stopped when we got around and had it out —one dyin big frosty snowball fight. It was a great bit of fun. It was cold all right, but I didn't mind that. All that snow coming down in those big, fat flakes. Lodging on my bare head and shoulders and gut and melting. Like I didn't give a shit about anything. And Curtis either and what the hell. It was some darn good.

When we gave it up, we was wet all right, not soaked now like you would be if it was raining, but still pretty wet in places. And cold! We got

what snow there was in the room out and then
hauled off the wet clothes and scravelled into the
sleeping bags. Cripes, it felt like it would take my
feet a week to thaw out. Not just cold, my son, like
the icicles they was.

"See, that was all your fault," I laughed and
shivered at the same time.

"Not the idiot, are you?" he said.

"Me, the idiot? My son, you're the one who
needs hes head examined."

And the feet freezing and us shivering and
laughing, all in those blessed arctic sleeping bags.

When we got up again, about an hour later, we
done it with a bit less of a fuss. I was right
anxious to see if the slips had anything in them,
so I couldn't stick it out in the sleeping bag any
longer. We both got up and hauled on the change
of clothes we each had brought along. Lucky
thing we did bring something, or we'd a been in a
bad state then. We hung up the sleeping bags as
best we could, to dry off a bit where the bottoms
of them got wet.

Once we was dressed and out moving around
we didn't find it near so cold. We grabbed a piece
of hard bread each to chew on and took off then
to where we set out the slips the day before.

It had stopped snowing and I could feel it
turning milder. What was on the ground probably
wouldn't last long. There was a coupla inches of
snow down in places, not really enough to cover

in the slips, but enough that they probably would need some fixing up. I had my fingers crossed that at least one rabbit found his way in before the snow got too deep.

Not only did one get in, but two more of his buddies too! In by the neck all of them, dead as doornails. And we only had ten slips out. Think what we might a had if we put out any more or if it had stayed clear all night. We'd a trotted home with a backload.

Holy dyin, three was plenty! More than plenty. That'd give us food enough for a good spell. Two of them was in slips I set out myself, the other in the one Curtis put out and I fixed up for him. He was a happy man all right—sorta his first rabbit in a way, with a little bit of help from me. He was no happier than I was, I tell you. Three rabbits in ten slips. Not bad atall. I hadn't lost my touch, even if it was inside a national park.

When it gets cold like it was that night before, then rabbits don't last long in the slips. Once they gets that wire around their neck and then starts struggling, well the cold starts wearing them down right away. If the wire is on nice and tight on the standard, then it ain't long before they're dead, out cold, stiff as a board. If it stays cold, then they'll keep like that in the slips a good while.

Sometimes, rabbits lying dead there in the slips can be a bad-looking sight. Some you gets, if they're caught by the hind legs, they'll have the fur chafed off the leg and the red flesh showing through. It don't look too nice. Some others might have parts eat off them, say, by a shrew or an owl. Some could be alive and you got to kill them. The most pitiful-looking thing I ever caught in a slip was a real young one one time. It was so small that I carried it home dead in my coat pocket. I didn't like it atall having caught something so small as that. I would a thought he was small enough to jump through the slip. But when that happens there's nothing you can do about it. You just got to put up with it and hope it don't happen again.

These fellows was all in by the necks. It took a bit of time getting the wire off from around them because it got caught up in the fur. We could a taken them snares and all, I spose, but I didn't want that. I'd string the snares out so no rabbits would get caught, but I wanted them left there on the standards. I couldn't very well fix them all up again and us with three rabbits already. If we caught any more the next day, we'd never be able to eat them. So I figured I'd string them out and then if we wanted to come back later on and set up for another feed, there'd be no problem. And by the looks of the tracks around in the snow, I knew there'd be plenty to catch.

We left the slips and walked on back then to the cooking shelter. We left two of them tied up inside the shelter, guts and all. They'd keep okay off the ground like that. Then it was the matter of cooking up the other one.

I gave Curtis his instructions on how to go

about skinning a rabbit, the way I learned it from Dad. It took two people the way we use to do it—one fellow to hold the rabbit by the hind legs, the other fellow to haul off the skin and gut him. The pocket knife I had was pretty sharp, not as good a knife as I'd like to've had, but it had to do.

While one fellow holds him up by the hind legs, you starts in skinning him there, working your way down to the head. The skin comes off inside out, like you'd peel off a tight sweater. You got to be careful with it though and know what you're doing cause you don't want to wind up with fur on the meat. The hardest part I always found to skin is around the head. That don't come off too easy, like in around the ears.

The guts'll drop out while you're doing it, but you should make sure to save the kidneys and the liver, and the lights too, if you likes them. They're some of the best parts. Once he's skinned, then you can cut him up—the hindquarters, the fore-quarters, the rib cage, the meaty parts down the back, and the head. You should always make sure to cut off and fire away the snotbox from the head.

That's it then. Curtis wasn't use to the blood and the bit of a stink, and I don't think he went too much on it, but he never complained. We washed the meat and our hands, and we was all ready then to start cooking. We had no pot, only tinfoil, so we couldn't make a real good job of it. And no pork fat or onions, that was the worst thing.

Nothing to give it that extra bit of taste. We just had to make do with what we had. It smelled good just the same, once we got it on the fire. We wrapped up a few spuds with some butter and tossed that over the fire along with it.

And later when we hauled it out cooked and sunk our chops into the meat, I tell you it was all right too. Not so good now as Mom could fix up with the onions and the salt pork, but pretty good considering what we had to work with. And then for a drop of tea. Only we had to settle for lousy old baker's loaf. That's enough to spoil a good dinner if you're not careful. Not half as good as the homemade, perhaps not a quarter.

But we made a feed out of it all, and a darn good one at that. No need to be ashamed of our cooking, that was one thing for sure.

18

Only for everything outdoors being so wet as it was, and the fact then that we had no more dry clothes, we might a gone off in the woods somewhere, away from the campsites altogether and fixed up a shelter out of boughs—a boughwiffen we calls it—and stayed there for the night. Just to get away from all signs of having to depend on someone for a place to live. Just to prove something, I guess. I might a wanted to do it, but I've got sense along with my stubbornness, so I figured it was best not to. Not this time, anyway. It wasn't that I couldn't a done it if I had to. But what was the sense of taking chances, especially when it got so cold in the nights.

So that afternoon we wasn't left with much to do. There was only so far we could walk without getting bored. We was done with rabbit catching for the time being. Fishing was outa the question that time of year. The fish would be too slubby to eat even if we did catch any. And the seven cans of Ajax and twelve packs of paper towels left in the janitor's place wasn't exactly the best things in the world to amuse ourselves with.

The only other thing that had been left in the room when we came there was a coil of nylon rope about thirty foot long. We had part of it tied up for a clothesline.

After a while of thinking it over, a second good use for it suddenly came to me. We rigged up a rope swing in one of the trees. You talk about the neat little outfit, my son, once we had it done.

I was a long while finding a sensible tree that we could tie it to—a tall one with no real big branches except up high. I could cut off any small ones with the axe I had. And the tree had to be out in the open so's we wouldn't bang up into any of the others when we swung around.

I shinnied my way up this spruce, cutting off the few branches as I went along, and then tied on one end of the rope where I thought it would hold good and solid. When I came back down to the ground, I tied the other end up in a few knots, so's we'd be able to get a nice tight grip on it. The way we had it rigged, you could leave this little hill when you grabbed onto the rope and then make a full swing right around the tree till you pitched back down on the ground where you started off.

I was on rope swings lots of times before, but as for Curt, I believe it must a been his first time. You could see by the way he swung off it that he probably never even seen one before. He never got out far enough and instead of swinging right around, he came back and rammed smacko, right into the tree. I never said anything. Almost killed himself, he did. Not really, but he gave himself a pretty hard goin-over.

After that, I didn't think he'd try it a second time, but in five minutes he was up at it again. This time I gave him a shove off and made sure he got away right.

Once he had the hang of it then, there was no giving up. He swung his guts out. Wonder he didn't chafe through the tree, he went around that many times.

It was a great bit of fun all right. In Marten, we use to have one something like that in by the pond summertimes, for swinging off into the water. What a time we use to have with it. You'd draw back, my son, and swing off from the bank as hard as ever you could go, trying to see who could pitch the farthest out in the water.

I guess you could say we glutted ourselves with swinging around that spruce tree. We was at it that long I was getting dizzy. It's some feeling, though, to be off on the loose like that, to have all your weight straining down on your hands around just a few knots on a piece of rope. Sometimes you figures, cripes, I'm going to fall, but you hangs on and after a while of being all loose and free, you finds that there you are landing right back down on the spot from where you left.

* * *

Well, to be honest about it, most of the second night we was bored stiff. There was nothing new left to do. It was dark by five o'clock and we played cards till we was blurry-eyed. And, when I thought about it, I knew there wasn't even a hell of a lot to look forward to the next day.

On top of that, I had it on my mind all that day about Brent and Aunt Flo and Grandfather. I knew they must a been worried sick by then. What was it—three days since we was missing? I knew Aunt Flo would be just about gone crazy if I didn't turn up soon.

So we agreed, right there on the spot, that the next morning we'd get up early and drive the car back to the parking lot and then thumb a ride to Marten. What would happen after that? Well, we'd just have to wait and see.

Once we had our minds made up to go, it seemed that we was all the more anxious to see the time pass. But we had nothing to rush around for and get done. It was only shove all our stuff into the knapsacks in the morning and take off. We had supper already—another rabbit. That left one hanging up in the shelter. I'd find something to do with that one in the morning.

By eight o'clock we was back at the cards again, trying to pass away the few hours until we was ready to go to sleep. A pretty dull racket. Except, that is, for the bit of a row me and Curtis got into. I spose you couldn't really call it a row. A misunderstanding was more like it. All caused by me having my big tongue going again.

Curtis was in the mood for talking that night. All the time since we'd come there he'd been in the mood for a good lot of stuff that he wasn't so hot on doing before. If someone had said two months before, when I first laid eyes on the guy, that we'd be there in the woods, laughing and carrying on like we'd done, I would a said they was nuts. Goes to show how much a fellow can change. Or perhaps it was just that he was having a chance at being himself.

He told me first that he didn't care whether we went or stayed. That he'd just as soon not have to face his parents for another week. I bet he must a been doing a lot of thinking about what would happen to him after we got to Marten. About his parents coming after him and all that.

"Maybe I could stay in Marten, eh, with you?" he said, pretty timid about the whole thing. We had the cards put away. We was lying down in the sleeping bags.

"You want to?"

"Sure."

"Cripes, but I don't even know what I'll be doing myself yet. One thing I do know for sure though, I won't be going back to St. Albert. They can make away with me first. I'm not even sure if Aunt Flo'll let me stay with her for frig's sake, let alone you too. I was thinkin of maybe stayin in our own house. Of openin it up again. Only I can't see where I'd get the money to pay for the food and the electricity and all that. I thought of cuttin wood and sellin it, but how much bloody wood would you need to cut to get that much money. I don't say I'd be able to get it to work."

"Maybe I'll have to go back home then."

"You care?"

"I guess I do. I don't know what to think. I can't run away for good. I guess I don't really want to anyway."

We both knew that what we was on wasn't running away from home and never coming back deals. We wasn't on the lookout for no circuses to join. We'd been out to prove something. And by then, maybe we'd done it.

"You know if I go back home it's going to be ten times worse with you not around," he said quietly.

I wasn't sure how to take that. "Maybe not," I said. "Maybe the old man's wised up in the last few days."

"I doubt it." Almost laughing, like it was a joke.

"Shit, you never knows."

"I hate to think what will happen if you're not there."

"Ah, whata ya after? You trying to flatter me up to get me to come back to your place? No way sir am I going back. No way. No matter what. Cripes, if you hates it that much why don't you leave it for good. I thought by now you'd have a little bit more guts at least."

"Guts! Frig off, Mike. You think it's that simple. Guts, guts! Frig, that's all you talk about isn't it. If I listened to you I'd just up and take off, never go back. You just remember it's my home, the only one I got, where I've been all my life. It's all right for you to talk. They're not *your* parents."

"Thank God for that!" I snapped back at him.

"Frig off, will you! Frig off! I know you got no use for them. But just leave it at that. They're the only bloody ones I got you know!"

"Ay, I'm sorry."

"Forget it."

"I really am."

"I said forget it. Okay!" he shouted.

He was mad at me, like I'd never seen him before. I knew I should never a said what I did.

We was in the sleeping bags, with just the light of two candles flickering around in the shadows. He turned on his side with his face in against the wall and we didn't say anything for a long spell. I didn't know what to say to him. It took a lot for him to get that mad. I guess I'd opened my mouth once too often. I thought I could put myself in his place and know what I'd do if I was him. Probably it wasn't as easy as I made it out to be.

He stayed there and stayed there, not moving.

"Hey, Curtis," I said after a while, "wanna have an arm wrestle?" I was gonna maybe let him win.

"Frig off."

That was brilliant on my part, wasn't it? Shit, sometimes I haven't got a clue.

I didn't try any more of the wise stuff. Even though I didn't much enjoy having him just lying there like that, I kept quiet and left things as they was. I knew what it's like being mad and people bugging you. The radio was on. I tried to settle down and listen to that.

After a long time, he turned over all of a sudden and spoke to me. "It's just that I don't know what's going to happen." It came out the same as if we'd never stopped the conversation at all.

I knew anything I said I had to be careful. "Is it because you're scared of your father?"

"No." Very quick.

"You sure?"

"No, I'm not scared. I think now it's like I got something to show that he can't always control everything I do anymore. And if he does get mad and turn savage on me, then he'll know that maybe I'll try running off again. I think I can stand up to him and say just what I think."

"Then whata ya worried about?"

"How things are going to turn out. What's going to happen between Mom and him. How we're all going to get along once I go back."

"It'll work out," I told him.

"Maybe."

"Sure you're not scared anymore. You'll face up to en, that's the main thing."

"No, it's not the main thing. If we're still not

going to get along, what bloody difference will it make if I ever go back." The way he was saying it so fast, I could tell he must a been thinking about it for a long time. "If I still can never talk to him except to fight and argue, then I might as well stay here and rot in these goddamn woods. Not being scared—it's not the main friggin thing at all."

19

We wasn't long in the sleeping bags, once I knew it was daylight. I wanted an early start. The sooner we got away and the less people that seen me driving the car the better.

Overnight it had turned off even milder and rained. The rain left most of the campground bare except for the scattered patches of snow under the trees. By the time it got light, the rain had stopped, but the sky was still dull and miserable. A good time to leave. Poor weather sending the campers home.

It took us fifteen minutes and we had everything cleared away and our knapsacks in the car. A few cookies and the last of the hard bread done for something to eat, a few mouthfuls of water for something to wash it down with.

The one rabbit left hanging up in the shelter—I hauled it down to go with us. I wasn't about to leave it there so that it would never be of any use to anyone. The rabbit slips could stay where they was. Strung out like that, they couldn't do any harm. Some mainlander camping there next summer would find them perhaps and tell a park warden and they'd be complaining about it for a few days and then it'd all be forgot.

That was it then. We had cleaned up around. We left the place pretty much like we found it. Going off in a rush because our minds wasn't on being there anymore.

Back on the highway there wasn't many cars on the go. Some came up from behind and passed, but not many head on to us. Like before too, the beanie pulled down over the head, the sunglasses on. I done around forty-five most of the way. On long stretches with nothing coming, a bit more. But no fancy stuff. You can't relax when you're driving and still have two and a half years to go to get your licence.

Only thing really on my mind was the time taking to get the car back where it belonged. In one piece. Back so that it could be parked there just like it never went anywhere in the first place. That it wasn't stole, just borrowed.

There I was—at it again. Trying to cover it up.

"Who we tryin to kid about stealin, Curtis?"

"What?" A far-off what.

"Never mind."

He was all in his own world. I felt sorry for the fellow. I knew what was going through his mind. I thought I knew what I would do in his place. Then, I was thinking, that's all right for you to say. You won't have to put up with it anymore. You haven't got to go back and face what's going to be there for him to face.

We made it, turned off the highway and down the road to the airport. Only thing was I fooled up on the last of it and went into the parking lot the wrong way. I drove in the exit. Darn it and all the arrows pointing at us. I had to stop, whip her in reverse and back up out of the parking lot, then go around and come in the right way. And then what, but the stupid spot where the car was left before was taken up. I had to squeeze her into the nearest one I could find. After a couple of weeks in England, though, Mrs. McKay wouldn't remember a little thing like where her car had been parked exactly.

Would you believe it? I banged into the rear of the car parked ahead of me. After going about a hundred miles and then to smack into someone on the last three inches. There was no dent or nothing on his bumper because we was going too slow. We checked. But just the idea of the thing—to fool it up on the last three inches.

We wasn't about to hang around the car for very long. We hauled out the knapsacks and put them on the ground. Then I dug out a scrap of paper from the glove compartment and wrote off a note saying that the key would be inside the terminal at the information desk. I put the note on the dash by the driver's side so that when she came she'd see it through the windshield.

What to do with the rabbit was the next question. No way could we take it with us, and you don't go around to strangers saying, "Hey you, you want a rabbit, a dead one?"

What I done was left it there in plain sight on the bonnet of Mrs. McKay's Volkswagen. Probably after we'd gone, someone came along and took it. Or maybe nobody did and maybe he rotted there on the hood of the car. Who knows. Maybe it rained and his fur got all matted together and he looked as ugly as sin crumpled up there. Maybe that's the way it happened and everyone who walked past the car was wondering what the hell this ugly rabbit carcass was doing on somebody's car. Looking and stinking like a pile of shit. Someone might a complained to the guard and he came out and scraped it off into a plastic bag. Turned the poor bugger of a rabbit right into a proper nuisance.

The key to the car I brought to the information desk. I told them it belonged to a Mrs. McKay and I made sure they wrote it down. I told them she would be coming in on a flight from England some time next week and she'd be coming to pick it up. Anybody might walk along and read the note in the car, so I said to buddy make sure the person's got an I.D.

We came right on then. No more fooling around.

We'd run into the same security guard again if we wasn't careful. We walked the mile and a half to the highway and stuck out the thumbs, both of us anxious to get the last of it over with.

It's tough to say just how I felt as the last car we got a ride with kept getting closer and closer to Marten. It was some kind of happiness about being back, but along with that was mixed up a whole lot of other things.

For fifteen miles after you turns down from the highway to get to Marten there's a stretch of nothing but trees and a few ponds. It seemed like forever getting through and to make things worse, the fellow that was driving the car and his wife who was with him knew who we was. They owned a grocery store in Spencer's Harbour, and they seen my face in their store a good many times before.

They was right full of questions, neither one of which I wanted to answer. I felt like telling them that it was none of their business, but the most I done was nod my head, mumble something, and make out I was too sick to talk. That would send the rumours flying when they got back home, needn't you worry, about me being sick. The old woman's mouth wouldn't leave the phone once she got inside her house.

Curtis, next to me in the back seat, hardly said a word, just like before. Hardly so much as a grunt.

It's hard to compare it to anything, what it felt like when we started seeing houses and saying to ourselves this is it, we're here. It wasn't much like any other time I ever came home. For one thing I never was away that long before. And for another, everyone was bound to have a load of questions, just like buddy and his wife who was giving us the ride.

We passed people on the road that saw my face and I wouldn't doubt turned around and stared their eyes out of socket after we was gone by. The fellow we was in with would a let us off at the intersection if it had been any other day with any other hitchhikers. But no, not this time. Just being nosey, he turned up the other road and stopped right in brest of Aunt Flo's gate.

I tried to make it look a bit normal, getting out of the car and opening the gate. I wanted to be inside the yard, at least, before all the commotion started. But I didn't have it open and Curtis didn't even have his knapsack out of the car when I seen the curtains move across the living-room window and Brent's face show up for about two seconds behind the glass.

Then I figured it'd start—the royal fuss. I could imagine the string of yells as one told the other, the holy lot of hurrying to get out the door and run and meet me.

But there was none of that.

As I came up the walkway, I seen Aunt Flo open the front door and I could see it was going to be worse than anything I ever dreaded. Her face was red and miserable from crying. I wished to God as hard as ever I could that somehow the meeting could be different.

She didn't come running like I expected and wrap her arms around me and squeeze the guts outa me and smother me with kisses all over my face. She only stood there in the doorway and tried to smile. Brent alongside of her, saying nothing, as if I was a brother he heard about but never seen before. Both of them making it all so tough on me coming home.

When I reached the door, she took her arms and put them around my shoulders and pulled me into her. Her eyes was filled up with tears.

It was all too hard and too much pain. I grabbed hold of Brent as I broke away and went into the house. I poked a few fingers into his ribs to wipe out the stupid business of moping around. Enough was enough.

"Hey you, I'm back again. No more peace for you, buddy. Your pest of a brother is back to torment the life outa ya."

He drew back, a bit of a smile came through, but nothing that made him look in the least bit happy.

"Oh, Michael," Aunt Flo said, "I've been so worried about you two. Where have you been? I was so sick with worry. Why in the world didn't you let me know you was all right? I thought you might be dead."

"It's all right. It's all right now. You knows me better than that. You knew I'd be all right."

"But why did you have to run away like that? Why did you have to go and not tell anybody? And Curtis, too. I spose his mother don't even know he's okay?"

"No."

"I've got to phone right now."

She rushed off down the hall to the telephone, leaving the three of us in the living room.

There was a stupid quiet. There was no need of it. I had to say to him, "So whata you been doin, eh Brent? Whata you been up to lately?"

"Nothin." He said it still like he had half his senses.

"What's wrong with ya? You looks to me like you're sick."

"Nothin."

I thought of it then all of a sudden that Grandfather wasn't around.

"Where's Poppy?" I asked him. "Down on the wharf?"

"He's in the room, in hes bed."

"Wha's he got—the flu?"

"No."

"What's wrong then? Hes back bad again?"

"No . . . the doctor says Poppy's dying. He says maybe he's got only two or three more days to live."

All this is dumb, friggin well dumb!

Two fellows runs away and then the best grandfather I ever could a had is dying on me.

I does stuff and not in a million friggin years do things work out. I'm forever left with something that I don't want to happen. I don't know why the hell we ever bothered to come back atall. We should a stayed in the friggin woods like Curtis said and rotted.

The whole friggin works of everything is screwed up. The whole friggin world.

And me trying to make some sense out of it. Not have myself messed up because still another person is almost dead. Trying to take it like the bloody brave ass I'm sposed to be. And how bloody far do I get?

I got nobody now here to help me. They're gone. And this is one time I don't figure there's enough of them left in me to hold fast.

20

I had seen an old person sick and dying before. It hasn't been that long since Grandmother Hodder died. But we all knew for a long time that it was going to happen.

As I walked down the hall to the door of Grandfather's room, a sick smell of liniment filled up my nostrils. I walked slower so I would get use to it. The door was partway open. I came to it, took hold of the old painted knob and pushed in. Except for the smell, the room was the way I remembered it. I knew the green palms in the wallpaper where the edges in some places didn't match. Every picture on the wall I knew. The ships and the old picture of King George. And the wooden model of the schooner on the bureau.

The bed with Grandfather in it. He was coughing and his body heaved up as I went in. He didn't hear my steps. He was lying with his back to me, his white hair the only thing that could be seen above the covers. I stopped and looked. His hair was longer than ever it was before, curled up in damp clumps on the back of his neck. He laid there, moving only when the coughing forced him to. His head sank back down on the pillow each time and he didn't stir.

I walked around the bed, to the other side where he would be able to see me. He didn't hear my footsteps still. His eyes didn't open. I looked at his face on the pillow and I seen how old and tired it was. He didn't look like the man who had me listening for hours to his stories. He wasn't the one I had seen hundreds of times heave a castnet and haul it to shore loaded with caplin. He wasn't the same fisherman atall.

I blinked water away from my eyes.

I sat down into the chair that was near his bed. It scraped across the floor. He stirred and his eyes opened. For a long time that was all he done—stare straight ahead at me. It took that much time for him to know who I was.

A smile spread across his face, to me as slow as the moon rising up out of the water. I wiped the tears out of my eyes and tried to smile back at him. He had to cough again, and it was gone, all his effort. He brought the crumpled-up handkerchief he had in his hand to his lips and wiped them.

"Grandfather," I said. My voice was too low, I knew. "Grandfather." Louder. It was hard being loud in a room so quiet. "Grandfather, I'm back."

I guess if he was sick Aunt Flo never told him

about me missing. To him, it was St. Albert I was
back from.

He moved his head slowly along the pillow as if
saying yes he knew. I lifted up the chair and
moved it closer to the bed so that I wouldn't have
to speak so loud. "I'm sorry to come back and find
you sick like this."

It wasn't easy to be doing all the talking, not to
have words coming back at you. Grandfather was
trying. He wanted to be telling me something
about how it was with him. The words that came
out was only mumbles, bits of sound that I tried
as hard as I could to make into sense. They didn't,
but I couldn't have him repeating them all again.

"Yes," I said, like I was agreeing.

It was hard on him. And it hurt me too, harder
than I ever let him know.

"Michael," I could remember him saying, "I can
mind the first time I was aboard a fishin schooner . . ." He'd talk then about the times they came
home loaded down with fish. And the bad times,
when luck wasn't so good, he'd talk about them
too.

He'd never be at it again. Maybe never even see
a boat no more. And for that, when I thought
about it, I could a cried a lot more.

He looked at me as if he knew what it was like
for me seeing him that way. He took his hand,
dragged it up to his head and grabbed onto a
bunch of his long hair, and made what he could of
a laugh. He was trying to make a joke out of it so

I would laugh. He was trying to make it easier for me. I had to smile.

"You needs a haircut," I said to him, like Aunt Flo use to be saying. "Going around like that. You should have better sense."

He smiled. I took hold of the hand that was resting by his stomach and held onto it tight. Then my head sank down on the edge of the bedclothes. He rubbed his other hand through my hair.

I rose up my head after a time to show him that the tears was all over and done with. Then when I squeezed his hand again that was the last time I touched him. The last time, ever.

Grandfather died three days later. He died finally when there was no way his body could take any more. It gave up on him. He had to pass away.

He was laid out in an open casket in church and buried the next day after that. I went to the service and sat up in the front seat of the church. In the cemetery I watched the casket go into the ground, never once did I move from the spot where I stood.

21

Only Brent and Aunt Flo and me was left then. Without a real lot of useless words between us, she understood that I was staying.

First when I came she wanted me to tell her all about the running away part. I knew she had a lot of right to hear reasons for it—she had worried and suffered her way through those three days and nights while we was just having a good time. But I was in no mood to be saying anything much about it. It was over, we was safe enough, I wanted to leave it at that.

But when Curtis' parents showed up that night after we got home I was forced into giving in a bit. They was looking for reasons too for what we'd done. Even so, what with Grandfather the way he was, I wasn't about to go out of my way with much of an explanation for Curtis' old man. And I didn't give a darn whether he liked that or not. It wasn't his own house he was coming into now. No good for him to yell and think I was going to jump.

The strange thing was though, when their car hauled up in the driveway and the two of them came through Aunt Flo's back door, they didn't look to me much like what they was before, not the picture I had in my mind since the morning we took off. I'll always remember it—the look they gave Curtis when they first came into the house. You'd think almost he was some kind of vision, the way they sized him up. Curtis across the kitchen sitting down at the table, both of them in the doorway not making a move, until finally Aunt Ellen ran across and hugged into him. Curtis hardly budged. He was stiff as a poker.

The old man. That was the one that was hard to figure out. He didn't open his mouth, not for the first five minutes after he came into that kitchen. That's true. He was lost for words. But really I should a known that even if the quiet wasn't a front then, it was bound to wear off.

It did. And later that night when we got down to the whys and hows and what thens, he was well on his way back to his old self. First he wasn't the big loudmouth like before, he was toned down a good bit. But when we started saying stuff he didn't like, then you could see his stupid old ways pushing right back through.

Old Curtis was a match for him though. He never gave him what he was looking for. Nothing close to it. I was some proud of that Curt.

We was all sitting down in the living room. Curtis was in an armchair by himself and his parents was across the room on the chesterfield. The first thing they brought up was why we had to take off like we done. I told them that it was my idea to go. And the reason—that I couldn't put up with living in their house anymore. I didn't mention anything at all about the school. And Curtis, he came out with it too.

"Mike didn't talk me into it, I decided my own self to go."

"But why, Curtis?" his mother said.

"Because . . . because I wanted some freedom for a change. I wanted to see if I could make it on my own."

They didn't know what to say to that. Until, in a few seconds, the old man came back with all this bull about how it was against the law. And then he says how he can't understand it, and what about everything they had? He didn't want to understand it, that was it. Not that he couldn't understand it atall.

Then it came to the part about us taking the car. It was something that I didn't really want to tell them, but Curtis sorta mentioned it by accident, so it all had to come out.

"That was stealing," the old man said. All along he was looking for something he could lash his teeth onto. He really had it then. "And you know what stealing makes you? It makes you thieves, boys. Nothing better than common criminals. You might as well pack your bags and get ready for reform school."

See, the bugger hadn't changed! Reform school! Shit, he was missing the whole stupid point! Sure it was stealing, I knew that, and maybe it was the wrong thing to do. But he stuck to talking about these couple of illegal things we done so's he wouldn't have to own up to the fact that he was the bloody reason we took off in the first place.

And the rabbits, that too. He made a bloody big case outa the three lousy rabbits we caught in a place where you wasn't sposed to put out snares. He almost gave us life sentences for three lousy rabbits. That's what friggin well got me mad.

But it was Aunt Ellen, not me, that cut him off. She said that was it. Now it was all over and now Curtis would be back home soon and they'd forget everything and start all over again.

But Curtis wasn't about to leave it at that. He had something that he wanted to get across to them, and he wasn't going to stop until it was done. He looked straight at his father.

"Not unless things change I won't be home long. I've been doing a lot of thinking about this..."

"What the hell do you mean 'unless things change'!" his old man butted in.

Aunt Ellen started to cry. I could see her eyes all watery. She didn't make any noise though, even when the tears started down her face. She wiped them away with her hand. The old man had to see what was happening, but that didn't stop him.

"Well, what do you mean!" he said again.

Curtis was still looking straight at him. "Dad, I never in my whole life ever said no to you. You had it so I was too darn scared. You had it so that I was afraid to even go near you half the time. But that's not the right way for it to be. Most of the time, I used to hate it as soon as I heard you walk into the house. I hated you. I still do now. Right now, this minute, I can look at you and see how much I hate you."

Curtis was staring at him. I never ever seen a look like that between two people.

"That's a rotten thing to be saying about your own father," Curtis said. "But you should know. I would like for it to change, but I'm not sure if it ever can."

The tension, you could chop it up with an axe if you had one, it was that strong. Nobody said anything. Curtis—he was waiting for something back from the other side. The old man—he was waiting too, not sure maybe what he should say. He wasn't about to let anyone in on the darn good shaking up his insides must a got.

He covered it up by turning the attention to Aunt Ellen. Now you could hear her cry. I almost expected him to say something dumb like, "Now, see what you've done," but there was none of that. All he done was try to calm her down. I spose that showed something.

"We'll talk about this when we get home," he said. "Ellen, stop crying now. We'll get everything straightened out when we get back home."

It was hard to say what he meant by "straighten out." Maybe what Curtis had said sunk in. Maybe he knew his bulldozer ways wouldn't have a hope in hell of working anymore. Only more time would tell.

It all ended there pretty well. From then to the time they left to drive home the day after the funeral, there wasn't much more said about it by either one of them. Curtis was off by himself or with me most of the time. And with Grandfather so sick nobody felt like talking much anyway, no matter how important it might a seemed.

It wasn't much of a good-bye what I said to Curtis when he left. It didn't seem like a time for one. When he got aboard the car to go, I figured it was enough that we just smiled at each other. We each knew anyway what the other fellow was thinking.

22

It's been two weeks now since the funeral. There hasn't been anything that I'd call normal in so long that I can't say that things are settling back to normal. They're calmed down a lot, though. The three of us, Aunt Flo and Brent and me, in the house is as good as ever it will be. I'm glad it's that way. We all miss Grandfather awfully bad.

I got a letter from Curtis. I don't know what's going to happen to him. From what he told me, it looks like nothing much is settled at his place yet. I thinks about his sister being in on it too. He said in the letter that his father hasn't done any yelling yet, but that mightn't mean much, maybe the worst is still to come. At least he didn't say anything about running away again, so perhaps some good has come out of all the racket.

He mentioned about Brenda. She was asking him about me. I'm going to write her as soon as I get chance. My mind hasn't had much room for her lately, but I know she'll be wanting to hear from me.

Right now I'm busy at Dad's skidoo out in the shed. Mine and Brent's I guess it is now. I'm trying to get her fixed up a bit before the winter comes.

Not that I'm over everything that has happened. But things like this skidoo here is helping me to forget how bad it was. The skidoo and Brent standing up there, me making it look like he's a big help. And Ronnie then and some of the other boys from up the road, that all sorta goes together to make a reason right now for doing things. For a while I can manage to put everything else out of my mind.

It's a real break to be able to do that, to get rid of all that emotional stuff for a while. To just have my mind on putting some grease on this machine, adjusting the carburetor, making sure the drive belt is okay.

I caught myself half on the bawl last night after I was in bed. There's still that time after every day when, no matter how much I've done, everything gets quiet and I'm alone with all that's happened and I feels like bawling. But I drove it out of my system last night and that might be the end of it. It was a hard bloody thing to do, but I thinks that maybe I got it done.